I0537979

Each year thousands of people make a spiritual journey called The Camino, an ancient walk through Europe, crisscrossing through France, Portugal and Spain. For two very different men, the trip has special dangers and, attractions. Antonio is one step away from becoming a transitional deacon, the final step before becoming a priest, but feels his new-found desire for other men violates his chosen vocation.

His nighttime dreams reveal a man he is passionate about, but to his amazement, he looks just like Zeb, a very handsome, mysterious man who is questioning things in his own life. How can Antonio be in love with someone who worships evil? And why is Zeb walking the path of The Camino?

The unauthorized reproduction or distribution of this copyrighted work is illegal. Criminal copyright infringement, including infringement without monetary gain, is investigated by the FBI and is punishable by up to 5 years in federal prison and a fine of $250,000.

This book is a work of fiction. Names, characters, places, and incidents either are products of the author's imagination or are used fictitiously. Any resemblance to actual events or locales or persons, living or dead, is entirely coincidental.

The Camino
Copyright © 2020 A.J. Llewellyn
ISBN: 978-1-4874-3025-2
Cover art by Martine Jardin

All rights reserved. Except for use in any review, the reproduction or utilization of this work in whole or in part in any form by any electronic, mechanical or other means, now known or hereafter invented, is forbidden without the written permission of the publisher.

Published by eXtasy Books Inc

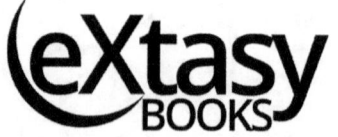

Look for us online at:
www.eXtasybooks.com or www.devinedestinies.com

THE CAMINO

BY

A.J. LLEWELLYN

DEDICATION

For Gina, whose spiritual journey to The Camino changed her life. Over lunch at the Inn of the Seventh Racherry, blossoms falling into our salads, the plotline for this book was born. Thank you for sharing your adventure with me and for allowing it to become the bones of Antonio's story.

Ciao, bella!

CHAPTER ONE

Antonio knelt on the floor a few feet away from the naked man who reclined in his leather-bound wooden chair, watching him. The man touched his cock with a languid hand. He smiled, beckoning Antonio who was mesmerized by the gorgeous man's long, tapered fingers, white even teeth and long, flowing hair.

Desire seemed to flare in the man's eyes, his gestures suddenly impatient. Antonio knew that *yes*, he wanted Antonio to suck him. Candles flickering around them, the only sound Antonio could hear was their increasingly short, sharp breaths.

Antonio held his breath. He loved the sound of the man's mounting passion.

"Do you want me to blindfold you?" the man asked as Antonio crawled toward him. It was difficult with his hands bound behind him, but all he cared about was getting his mouth around the cock bobbing in front of him.

"No. I want to look at you."

The man shook his glossy brown hair, his eyes darkening with lust as he looked down at Antonio. He scurried across the last remaining inches of floor space, earning a smile from the man in the chair.

Just an inch away now, Antonio held his mouth open. He was close enough to drink in the finer details of the gorgeous man's dusting of chest hair. The man scooted forward just a little in his huge, kingly chair, anxious for the cock to mouth contact.

1

Antonio had thought he might want to be blindfolded since he was so shy about being naked, and with another man, but was surprised to find being bound was enough. He wanted to be able to watch the man's reactions as he sucked him. He licked his lips. He couldn't wait.

He reached the edge of the leather seat. The smell of leather and warm, manly skin went straight through him and to Antonio's cock.

The man before him moaned, bit his lip, jutting his hard cock forward until it touched Antonio's now wet mouth. He allowed his cock to slide across the full, lush lips. They looked deeply into each other's eyes.

"Open," the man whispered, and Antonio did as he was bid, sucking in the biggest cock he'd ever seen in his life. Raising himself a little higher on his knees, he worked hard to suck as much of the cock into his mouth as he could. He blinked. He thought he might choke but the man whispered words of lust, sweet words of encouragement.

Fuck.

Antonio could taste the bittersweet syrup from the other man's cock. He was aware of his own cock hardening. It was such delicious torture not to be able to touch it. Not that he needed to. He always came, especially when the man lifted his cock away from Antonio's mouth and begged for him to tongue his ass. It never failed. Antonio closed his eyes, his mouth descending to the other man's special, private place and—

Damn.

He came.

Antonio opened his eyes. A wave of sadness washed over him, even as he experienced such savage relief from masturbation. Fear consumed him momentarily as he took in the unfamiliar surroundings. Where was he? Oh, yes, Mount Calvary at St. Mary's Benedictine Monastery and Retreat House.

He held onto his softening shaft to prolong the euphoric

feeling, careful not to brush the sensitive head. He remembered to breathe, then smiled. *Wow*. The fantasy of the man in the chair always ignited his passions. He longed to delve deeper into pleasuring his nameless, faceless lover but he could never get that far. The newly discovered bliss of self-gratification had come with myriad emotions. Being bound in his fantasy absolved Antonio of responsibility for his actions. In his mind, anyway. It also fueled his fire more and more he found.

Completely unsuitable thoughts and behavior for a man destined for the priesthood, Antonio realized. He had denied himself for so long, but at the age of twenty-four, it had come as a shock, and a blessing. He released his cock and turned over on the small bed.

His room was large and contained mostly functional, but comfortable items and yet it still seemed a lot more luxurious than his usual quarters at St. John's Seminary in Camarillo. The vase of thick branches of rosemary entwined with lavender roses, on his bureau, gave the room a heavenly smell as well as a touch of warmth.

Antonio lay with his arm under his head, listening to the sounds of the unfamiliar monastery. All was still and quiet as it was supposed to be. Restless, he swung his feet over the edge of the bed and stared out of the window of his private quarters.

He wondered if anyone ever broke the vow of silence of Mount Calvary. It was almost eight p.m. Soon it would be sunset, and the official Great Silence would descend over the property like a heavy blanket until the following morning. Already he chafed. Silence! All he ever got was silence. And austerity. Why had Monsignor Loftus suggested a sabbatical here when Antonio longed to talk and talk, and for good measure, *talk*?

He stared at the lush grounds with their unusual trees, the

beautifully tended gardens and surrounding them, the magnificent mountains of Santa Barbara. He could hear the ocean waves crashing at the foot of the cliffs. Yes, it was stunning. This was supposed to be a brief respite before returning to St. John's Seminary, but he'd known the second he'd arrived here that this life wasn't for him. The old Monsignor had been smart in directing him to Mount Calvary. The life of a priest would mean a lot of silence. A lot of contemplation.

He'd already told the Monsignor in a phone conversation that morning that he needed more time. The Monsignor had agreed, suggesting he take a month off. He'd even thrown out the idea of The Camino.

Antonio had heard of it but had only been able to look it up online for a few minutes in the monastery's business office. His cell phone, laptop, and iPad had all been confiscated from him when he arrived.

What they gave him in exchange was silence.

And a vow of silence was not what Antonio Duschene needed. He was ready to jump out of his skin. He needed to talk. He needed voices and people.

He'd said this to Monsignor Loftus who had said, "Antonio, you need to rediscover your faith. I have no idea when you became vulnerable, but The Camino is a wonderful journey. You'll meet so many new people. You will walk The Way of Saint James and rediscover your inner strength."

He sounded so confident that Antonio almost believed him. He would walk The Camino. He and Monsignor Loftus had made an agreement. Antonio would take a longer break of thirty days. He would go to Spain and take the sacred, spiritual pilgrimage hundreds of thousands of people took each year. At the end of it, he'd return to the seminary to prepare for his next steps to the priesthood, starting with his mission as transitional deacon.

Antonio had been alone with his thoughts long enough to

know that this was when his problems had started. Monsignor Loftus had told Antonio that the next part of his vocation would take place in Alabama.

Alabama! He had no desire to go to Alabama. He felt adrift just thinking about it. And yet here he was planning a trip to Europe, the details of which were to be his own decision. It was the first time in the four years since he'd joined the seminary that he could make his own decisions. He reveled in the slight decadence of that feeling. Freedom. It was sweet.

He wondered if he should call his parents and let them know of his plans. No. They had been against his career choice from the beginning and would undoubtedly suggest a family trip to The Camino. He could just see it now. Photos at every turn, long, newsy emails back to their friends and family members scattered around the world.

Antonio blushed when he thought about the fact that his mother had wanted him to be a fashion model, following in her footsteps. Sure, some might say he had the looks with his blond hair that had a tendency to curl and blue eyes that revealed every nuance of mood, but Antonio had chosen the priesthood.

Now, he just didn't know. He didn't want to alert his parents and have to deal with their hysteria if he decided to return to St. John's. They didn't even know he was here. The last email he'd received from them had a been a week ago. They were vacationing in the Florida Keys and had been disappointed when he declined to join them.

He turned his mind to his own plans. He would be leaving in two days. Now he had to plan his journey, for there were many paths he could take. He knew the most popular path went from France to Spain, but which would help him rediscover his faith . . . or lead him to the path he was supposed to take for the rest of his life?

Antonio let himself out of his bedroom. He shared a

bathroom with a man whose room was to his right. To his surprise, he saw his neighbor had checked out. Antonio had learned that three thousand overnight stays had been booked in the past twelve months. Lots of Californian rich hippie types booked Mount Calvary as an alternative holiday experience. It was listed as one of the top ten spiritual retreats in the whole of the United States, and one of the top fifty romantic getaways. The man at the front desk had told him this.

Some people came and appreciated the mountaintop retreat, the rigid daily schedule, the rustic meals, the sound of prayers and the enforced quiet. Unfortunately, some people expected a more commercial spa experience. Still others, like Antonio needed noise. And haste. Mount Calvary made as much money from people who came and ran away from the peace and quiet as it did from people who genuinely craved the stillness.

How weird, Antonio thought. The ancient saints too, had needed silence for contemplation and found it, just by seeking it. Today, people paid for it. A lot. As a seminarian, he'd received a slightly reduced rate but the path to peace came with a hefty price tag. You could get anything, even divine intervention with a credit card deposit.

In his bathroom, he checked his watch. He'd missed supper. He hurriedly washed his face and hands, cleaned his teeth and went downstairs for compline, the final prayer service for the day. He didn't particularly want to pray.

He just wanted permission to make noise.

After the brief service concluded, he wandered outside the church and the other outlying buildings. Lights blazed in about half of the twenty-four guest room windows. The solitude felt right for the first time since he'd arrived. He took a seat on porch swing, then hastily got to his feet when it made a squeaking noise.

Antonio wandered the grounds, excitement mounting in

him. As he turned and studied the drop-dead gorgeous Pacific Ocean looking dark and dreamy at the bottom of the mountain, he realized he'd made the right decision. The waves crested in foamy, brilliant white caps, making him think of the man from his dreams.

It frustrated him that everyone he asked had a different opinion on his erotic dreams. A few of his friends in the seminary said it was normal. A few older ones acted alarmed. St. John's had suffered tremendous blows with some of its long-time graduates being accused of child molestation.

He hadn't asked the Monsignor's opinion. Nor was he likely to. Whether he pursued a religious life, or not, when he made his final choice it would come upon great deliberation, with no recriminations and no regrets.

Antonio felt certain that one way or another, The Camino would show him his own path to peace. He rushed – in silence – to his room, anxious to be alone with his secret, shadowy lover.

The Great Silence lasted through breakfast, a meal Antonio raced through until he could get into the office and check the online information for the walk. For an hour, he read as much as he could and decided to take the most popular walk, The Camino de Santiago, which was also known as the French Way. It was the original route and now over a hundred thousand people took this way each year. He chose it because he wanted human contact and because the French Way had the most choices available in hostel accommodations and cafes to eat. He jotted hasty notes.

There were other, less busy routes, but this felt right to Antonio. His chosen way was over 778km long. He calculated this in miles and it worked out to be about 483. The walk took place over several stages. It started in Saint-Jean-Pied-de-Port, or St. John at the Foot of the Pass, on the French side of the

Pyrenees mountains bordering Spain. The route passed through picturesque, once abandoned, ancient towns such as Pamplona, the first official town of The Camino, Puente la Reina, Estella, Logroño, Burgos, León, Astorga, Ponferrada and Sarria, ending in Santiago.

If he chose to start at the second stage in Spain, the route would apparently take him four weeks. If he started in France, he could still possibly make it in the same amount of time, but it could possibly take two weeks longer.

He decided to start in France. He wanted to do it all. He felt he couldn't set a time limit on his spiritual renewal. Besides, Saint-Jean sounded like a lot of fun. Pamplona was famous for its annual Running of the Bulls festival. Funny how such a cruel sport got more world-wide attention than a spiritual walk.

Antonio had to obtain a pilgrim passport, whatever that was. He became almost dizzy with information, walking tips, packing tips, and realized he needed to leave Mount Calvary as soon as possible if he was going to acquire everything he needed in a timely manner.

Antonio read of The Camino's history. Ancient pilgrims took the walk as a test of faith. They took it because it was difficult. They endured deprivations, attacks, thefts and beatings. Today's pilgrim had it easier. Antonio studied all the blogs and numerous websites covering the trails. He envied YouTube images of couples holding hands as they walked, of the laughing families traipsing through country roads dotted with brightly colored wildflowers.

He took note of all the advice on packing light and purchasing the right hiking boots. The beauty of the French Way was that anything he'd forgotten he could buy along the trail. He liked the idea of the walking sticks some people used. He could buy those along the way, too.

Yes, this walk was the right thing for him.

The first thing he said aloud since the previous day was, "I am so sick of being alone."

Zebediah stood in the shadows of a cluster of ironwood trees outside an abandoned house on the curve of a cul-de-sac. He gazed up at the brilliant blue sky of a late July afternoon. No hint of sunset, no *obvious* sign of trouble, but he'd been sent here for a reason. It bothered him that the two children playing across the road outside their family home, had been un-supervised by an adult for at least fifteen minutes.

The five-year-old boy, Timothy, was doing a very good job of watching over his three-year-old sister, Ginny, but still, it was a job no child of five should have to deal with.

"No, Ginny, like this," Timothy said, helping his sister put the training wheels onto her pink bicycle. Zebediah glanced up at the top of the street. The non-descript white van was getting ready to make a long slow circle down the cul-de-sac again. The driver was careful to hold a piece of paper in his hand, pretending to look for an address.

Yeah, right. The street, located in a remote section of rural Michigan had more abandoned homes than any other Zeb had ever seen. Foreclosures were rampant, the scent of misery strong, despite the sunny day. An almost empty street gave parents a false sense of security. It was ludicrous. Summer va-cation was peak shopping time for pedophiles. How many children needed to be snatched in the blink of an eye before parents realized they could never trust the streets outside their doors?

Zeb knew the driver wanted the little girl. Her last mo-ments on Earth would be terrifying. The driver looked furious that Ginny had such a protective older brother. The little boy helped push his sister along the cracked sidewalk as far as the house next door, before insisting on returning to the space outside their family home.

In another minute, the little girl would be gone.

Ginny pedaled faster, the pink and white streamers of her handlebars flaring as she rode. Timothy lost his grip on his sister's bike. He fell, hard, on the sidewalk, his chin bouncing off the cement. Timothy looked stunned. It took him a second to react. He saw his own blood pouring from his mouth onto the sidewalk and he started to cry.

"Timmy!" the little girl shouted.

Zeb couldn't stand it. It was too cruel. Timothy's life would be ruined. He would never get over witnessing his sister's fatal abduction. Zeb zapped himself inside the disheveled house. The children's mother had a stack of laundry waiting in baskets beside an ironing board. She was watching TV, waiting on the phone to purchase gaudy jewelry on the Home Shopping Network.

"Come on, come on," she muttered, leaning forward on the sofa as the jewelry selections still available for purchase wound down in a small box on the left-hand corner of the screen. "Three left!" she yelled, at the exact same moment her daughter shrieked for her outside.

"Fuck!" Zeb screamed at her. "Run!"

He broke protocol without hesitating and picked up the remote, flinging it at the screen door.

"What the . . ." the woman stared at the door, saw the van idling outside in her driveway and got up from her sofa.

Zeb zapped himself outside again just as the driver jumped out of the van, approaching the little girl who'd dropped her bike to run toward her brother.

"Hey!" the woman yelled. The man's gleam of anticipation vanished from his otherwise empty eyes. He backed away.

The woman stepped out front, grabbed her daughter and ran to her little boy who was on his knees now. The driver muttered something about trying to help. They all vanished as Zeb found himself hurtling through space and landing hard on a wooden floor. His face mashed into the fitlhy . . .

Uh-oh.

He was inside the empty house across the road. The odor of rat droppings and something else filled his nostrils. Oh, yeah. Matthias. He always smelled like shit.

A foot came down hard on his head. A cloven foot at that. Nice touch.

Zeb reached up a hand as Matthias bent down to him, and he grabbed the foot, hurtling the ancient demon across the room. Matthias landed against the wall, not expecting the assault. Zeb was on his feet in seconds. He stood, in human form, unbowed by what he knew was about to be a severe punishment.

Matthias, his Watch Commander, advanced toward him, in full demon mode.

"You had your chance, Zebediah."

Zeb shrugged. "You bated me."

Matthias paced the room, apparently awaiting instructions. What Zeb had said was true. Temporarily stripped of his powers as a storm demon, Zeb had been given a second chance as a Watcher. A Watcher watched. A Watcher didn't intervene and save children from their predestined fate.

Obviously, Matthias wasn't being given permission to annihilate his nemesis. Zeb wouldn't have minded an eternity of rotting in hell, but thanks to his father's transgressions, he'd been given a more active role. A role he'd hated but had undertaken to try and repair the damage his father had done.

Actually, what he wanted was to be free. To be human. Man, that life seemed like centuries ago . . . What had gone wrong wasn't his fault. Assigned a new position as a Watcher, he still couldn't manage to stay out of trouble.

Matthias turned and talked to someone behind him. Zeb could just make out the shadowy images of the Unholy

Alliance. The three hastily assembled demons were about to pass judgment on him again but preferred to remain incognito. Groovy.

"Bunch of wusses," he muttered. "If you're about to crucify me, you should show yourselves."

Matthias, who hated Zeb for reasons unknown, said, "Crucifixion's too easy for you, Zeb. Let's see if this teaches you a lesson." He drew back his hand and came back with a fireball. Next thing Zeb knew, he sprawled on his back, dozens of men running over and beside him. He got to his feet, turning at the sound of screaming voices.

Shit. *Bulls!*

They were running right at him. He turned around again and started to run. It all happened so fast. He found he was on a narrow, cobblestoned street, tall, pastel painted buildings on either side, lined with people who apparently thought he was trying to get away from the bulls when he tried to bust through the crowd. They were right. They jeered and swore at him in Spanish as they pushed him back into the street.

Spanish.

Holy crap.

He was in Pamplona in the middle of the Running of the Bulls.

Zeb tried zapping himself out of the frenzied action, but found he had no juice. Swell. Now he'd been stripped of all his powers. But for how long?

He felt the horns of an ornery bull right on his ass and dodged to his right. The bull's wild-eyed stare told him the poor, dumb creature was petrified but also capable of killing him due to his sheer size. It was a brown and white bull, destined he knew, for a terrible fate.

Zeb got away from the bull. Wasn't it Hemingway who'd written, "He who hesitates is lunch?"

Somehow Zeb managed to weave his way around the massive animal, then three more of them as they charged the runners, the crowd booing its displeasure with him. Dozens of people on balconies, cameras in hand, gave him the finger. They wanted to see blood. Zeb took off again, skimming the street-side crowd, crouching low. He'd read somewhere that if you go down, stay down.

He got between two people's legs and got a bit of breathing room. Voices crowded in his head. It was the first time in a long time that he actually felt scared. He had no idea what was happening to him. He tried to stay low, but one of the men in the crowd grabbed Zeb by the back of his shirt collar and threw him back into the melee.

Zeb hit the cobblestones and glanced at the feet of the man who'd grabbed him. Cloven. Goddamned Matthias.

More bulls came. Zeb took off running again. Ahead of him to his left, the bull he'd seen earlier, was goring some guy on the ground. The guy screamed as the bull impaled him with a horn.

As others tried to get past the horrible scene, bulls and the runners became log jammed. Down the hill ahead of him, Zeb saw the open bullring waiting for the bulls. The stands were packed. All of the bulls would find their way in here to be slaughtered by matadors.

This was the most dangerous moment, Zeb knew. The final, dramatic, congested moments could bring death to any of the runners. He took off to his right just as a herd of bulls stampeded the last hundred yards into the bull ring. Zeb heard somebody scream and turned to find a young man tumbling beneath their rampant hoofs.

Zeb slumped against the wall beside him and watched. He felt shaky and sick. He hadn't felt any of these human symptoms since he'd made his offer to the devil. Something told him he hadn't been released from his contract. He had a feeling it had just gotten a thousand times worse.

He felt in his pockets, examined his attire. He wore jeans, a new-torn shirt, running shoes and . . . no wallet. He was in Pamplona with no money, no identification, and no way out.

"Who's the wuss now," a deathly voice rasped in his ear.

Zeb started. He could smell Matthias's foul breath, but the demon vanished. Zeb let out a sigh. His stomach started to rumble. For the first time since his horrible ordeal had begun, Zebediah felt hungry.

He had never been to Pamplona. He'd never been to Spain. His knowledge of the language was rudimentary. He was so hungry he was ready to steal. He saw a couple getting up from a table at a small sidewalk cafe and slip backpacks over their shoulders. The man left a half sandwich on his plate. There was a bread roll in a basket.

"Can I have your sandwich?" he asked the man, who turned and looked at him.

"It's not very good," the man said. Zeb was stunned to find they'd both spoken in fluent Spanish. How had Zeb managed that?

The man handed him the plate. He said, "I am sorry you are hungry," and then he and the woman took off. Zeb took the sandwich from the plate, and feeling the gazes of others around him, tried to merge with a stream of travelers passing by the cafe.

He walked around the square, chomping on his sandwich. The man had been right. It wasn't very good. It looked inviting but tasted very bland. Zeb consumed it, however. In his circumstances, he couldn't afford to pass up free food. He ate, his gaze going everywhere. He could see ghosts, he could read things about people passing by him. He still had some of his other-worldly senses, he just had no power.

Zeb finished the last bite of bread. The pickles in the last portion had tasted sour. Oh, man, this was how his trials had begun. Food had begun to taste weird. The devil wasn't done with him yet.

He walked around, listening to people in a variety of languages. They all seemed to be here for The Camino. He knew this was some kind of pilgrimage, some kind of walk. He didn't feel like walking, that was for certain. He had no idea beyond the Running of the Bulls why he was here. He'd survived that. He heard a shout of joy coming from the bullring.

As he peered into the windows of some of the small shops in the square, a few minutes later he saw a horse-drawn cart come by with the pathetic remains of a slaughtered bull. He watched, the bull's head lolling to the side, his eyes open, death only recent. The animal's neck and shoulders were covered in ribboned lancers that spoke of a tortuous death, with its arteries slowly severed, rendering him immobile.

Why am I here? I don't want to be here. I don't want to feel pain and suffering. This is a worse kind of hell than the one the devil owns.

For the first time since he'd made his pact with the devil, the questions that had haunted him began to resurface in his mind. The devil could think what he liked. Zeb had no regrets about saving the little girl . . . or her brother. The truth was, it was Timmy he'd sought to save. No child should spend the rest of his life punishing himself for something way out of his control.

Zeb found himself standing outside a store when a couple blew past him. The man dropped his wallet from the top of his overstuffed backpack. Zeb stared at it a moment and made a split-second decision. He moved over to it, covering it with his foot. He could call them and alert them to the dropped wallet, or, he could take it and use whatever was inside it for himself.

He bent down to pick it up and when he rose again, he could no longer see the couple. He thought he spotted them up ahead and went after them. When he caught up with the man, however, it wasn't the right one. The man in front of him turned and something happened to Zeb as their gazes locked.

He read so many things about the man in the small moment.
The most astonishing one however was . . .
  Priest.

CHAPTER TWO

Antonio looked into the green eyes of the most handsome man he'd ever met. He shook his head when the stranger held up the wallet.

"It's not mine," he said.

The stranger kept staring at him. His long, dark hair was like a mane. There was something almost . . . unreal about him.

"I'm Zebediah," the stranger said.

"Antonio." They shook hands, probably longer than necessary, but no, it was *very* necessary. Antonio heard the stranger say something, but a shout went up. The bullfights were in progress. Strangers jostled them and he lost physical contact with the handsome man. Antonio found himself trying to spot the dark-haired man but couldn't as a huge group of people stampeded past him. Antonio tried hard not to feel aggrieved. He'd first encountered this same group on the Air France flight from Los Angeles to Paris. He had already been stressed out from having shelled out a lot of money for the flight. There'd been cheaper deals but the Turkish Airlines flight which would have been roughly half the Air France fare involved a stopover in Istanbul and would mean that Antonio would be traveling for a full twenty-four hours without being any closer to The Camino's starting point.

The eighteen people now marching past him were the type that gave American travelers poor reputations. They were part of a twelve-step program and thought their sobriety was such a big deal they actually shouted at a honeymooning couple across the aisle who dared to order glasses of red wine on board the flight. The young couple looked bewildered, but encouraged by other passengers, they'd continued sipping at their wine.

Oh, yes. The twelve-steppers had intimidated a lot of people.

Antonio still shuddered remembering the fuss one of the group had made about his onboard meal, shouting at the dainty flight attendant about the *coq au vin* having wine in it. Antonio, who'd been sitting opposite the man had resisted the urge to say, "*Coq au vin* means chicken cooked with wine. What did you expect?"

The argument went on. Antonio had been dumfounded by the man's ensuing tirade, which became so vociferous, he began to wonder if this particular twelve-stepper was actually drunk.

At the Eurail station in Paris Gare de Montparnasse, he'd encountered the group again. This time they'd all gone nuts because they hadn't done their homework and didn't realize the company's France-Spain rail pass package could not be purchased in Europe. It had to be purchased online in the US and could be collected once they arrived in Europe. As Antonio waited for his early morning train to St. Jean Pied-du-Port, he'd been dismayed to discover they were also going to The Camino. They'd ganged up on him having recognized him from the flight.

He had held onto his pass a little bit tighter as they peppered him with questions. They'd also latched onto the lone ticket seller shielded behind the bars of his booth. He had no idea where St. Jean Pied-du-Port was. The twelve-steppers were frantic to reach the town that day.

Antonio had no clue what to tell them. He was planning to go to St. Jean Pied-du-Port, see something of the town, spend the night, then head off the following day to Roncesvalles.

Antonio had been so relieved when another traveler told them they could also reach the town by bus. That had been four days ago and now they'd finally caught up with him in Spain.

Antonio loved what he'd seen so far of The Camino. St. Jean Pied-du-Port had been as beautiful as everyone had said it was. They had issued him a pilgrim passport and stamped it, warning him to get a good night's sleep because his first day's walk would be rough.

Each place he visited he had to remember to get his passport stamped to prove he'd walked The Way, and that he therefore qualified to stay in an *albergue.*

His first day had been grueling. Nothing had quite prepared him for how physically taxing the walk would be, in spite of the warnings. He'd seen several elderly people leaving earlier and wondered how they could possibly cope. The path was all almost entirely uphill.

When he did stop and smell the flowers, he had to admire God's handiwork. The mountains were spectacular. He half expected Fraulein Maria to burst out along the way, arms outstretched singing, *The Hills Are Alive with The Sound of Music.* He got hot, tired, thirsty and hungry, and somehow, he'd lost his favorite wide-brimmed hat in the hostel that first night. He suspected it had been stolen. Ironically, he'd been told that St. Jean Pied-du-Port was the least safe portion of the journey. Sleeping there certainly hadn't been fun. His bed was uncomfortable, and it had no sheets. He soon learned this was often typical.

Now in Pamplona, he was keen to start walking but he'd been warned by the staff at the *albergue* that unless he got a very early start he might have trouble securing accommodations in the next town of Roncesvalles.

He'd walked from the tiny market town tucked in the hillsides of the great Pyrenees soaking everything in, but fourteen miles, most of it uphill was harder than he'd imagined.

There were times in the heat of the day that he'd berated himself for his need to commune with nature. He'd slept hard, both from the long walk and jetlag.

He had taken the advice of an online blog, woken early, showered and dressed and walked in the direction of Roncesvalles. He was tickled to find everything the blogger said he would. Wild barking dogs just a few miles into his walk and a fantastic little town, Espinal, which served the best breakfasts for travellers on The Way. After a hearty repast of crusty bread with chunks of ham and cheese washed down with gigantic cups of coffee, his second day's walk from Roncesvalles to Larrasoana had been almost perfect.

Ironically, it was longer than the first day at sixteen miles, but it was downhill for the first portion of the journey. It was in Larrasoana that he met a Franciscan monk, whose name was Theodore. His story seemed to similar to Antonio's. He was from Baltimore and this was his third Camino. He'd done two of the more obscure trails and said he'd taken a rest and was now tackling the French Way.

They'd walked together the last five miles, arriving in the beautiful but very rural Larrasoana, got their pilgrim passports stamped, but found the hostels were all full. Theodore spoke fluent Spanish and secured them a room for the night at one of the private farm homes that enjoyed a little cash on the side by taking in weary walkers.

The room had been tiny, and the two men laughed over their rudimentary cots in a small space off the kitchen. Theodore spoke fluent Spanish and laughed when he overheard the farmer telling a neighbor that he had put the two men in a small room where he could keep his eye on them. He didn't trust either of them around his wife.

That had made both Theodore and Antonio laugh since

they were both gay, but the fantastic breakfast the following morning of homemade bread and honey went a long way to make up for any inconvenience their uncomfortable beds had caused.

From the minute he'd arrived in Pamplona the night before, he felt something shift. Theodore had left without a word at the crack of dawn. He had said the night before that he was meeting up with friends at the next stage, Puente la Reina. Having walked with the man for a day and a half, Antonio had become very comfortable with him. He couldn't help feeling disappointed that Theodore couldn't even say a simple goodbye.

Antonio had been discomfited by the Running of the Bulls and the knowledge that these warrior-animals faced grisly deaths in the ring.

He overheard one of the twelve-steppers arguing with somebody, but Antonio had lost sight of them. Not that he minded. Hopefully he wouldn't run into them again. Maybe he should grab a coffee and let them move ahead. He wondered if Theodore had caught up with his friends then wondered why he cared.

Just as he was about to walk to one of the many cafes, he noticed a wallet on the ground. He picked it up. He tried to recall where the *albergue*, or pilgrim's hostel, was that he'd spent the previous night. He found it easily. The walls of all the hostels were marked with ornamental shells. He entered the office, but they were swamped. When he handed the wallet in, the man behind the counter opened it. The wallet was completely empty. No ID, no cards, no cash, nothing. He shot Antonio an accusatory glare.

"I found it like that," he said in his rudimentary Spanish. He was trying hard to learn more via lessons he'd downloaded onto his iPod. He listened to them as he walked. Since he'd met Theodore he'd stopped the lessons. Now, he would start again.

The man shrugged and tossed the wallet into a plastic basket with a bunch of other lost items.

"My hat!" Antonio said. Again the man gave him a suspicious look but Antonio had sewed labels with his name on them into all his clothing at the seminary. Since the tag in the hat matched the name in Antonio's passport, the man had no choice but to hand it over.

Antonio turned and noticed the handsome, dark-haired stranger with the green eyes passing by the office. He hurried outside but the man was gone. What was his name? Zebediah? It was such an unusual name.

He looked up and down the busy square. He really didn't feel like walking. He had a fourteen mile stretch ahead of him. He knew there was a little village over the first downhill ridge called Cizur Menor. He'd read that as he entered the village he would see a pharmacy and two cafes on his left. Apparently, these cafes were the last spots of civilization for the rest of the journey to Puente la Reina. He suspected they might be packed with Wayfarers. On the other hand, he'd missed the breakfast rush so he might find a table before the lunchtime crowd descended on the area.

Antonio longed for coffee. Well, he also longed to get away from the bull fights. He only had a few miles to walk until he reached Cizur Menor. From what he'd read, it was pretty but very rural so breaking up the walk a little made sense. He should get started though.

So why wouldn't his feet move?

The truth was he was hoping to spot the intriguingly named Zebediah. He scrunched his toes in his boots, jostling his backpack to a more comfortable position on his shoulders. He had brought two pairs of walking boots and a pair of running shoes. His feet had hurt the first day and now with two pairs of socks inside his boots seemed to do the trick. He felt a blister starting on the back of his right heel and decided to ignore it. Maybe it would go away.

He'd bought a pair of walking poles as soon as he'd arrived in Roncesvalles and he found that wielding them as he walked put him into a kind of meditative state.

The walk to Cizur Menor was easy, mostly downhill and he had to admit, the view of the road beyond was alluring. He felt himself entering the meditative space he'd been in before he'd encountered before he'd met Theodore. Maybe he was meant to embrace the Great Silence after all. He caught himself up short. He could almost hear the Mother Superior from *The Sound of Music* warning the novice nun Maria that the convent was not a hiding place for people.

Antonio passed a church that could have come straight from the movie and stood, admiring it. According to his guidebook, the Iglesia San Miguel Archángel had been built in the thirteenth century. He touched the heavy, ornate, gothic wooden door, imagining the ancient pilgrims who might have sought refuge here. He read that in ancient times it was a fortress. In more recent years it had been used to store grains. Now it was a fully functioning church again. He was able to open the door and walked inside. It had pink limestone flooring and a tombstone in the middle of it made out of the same pink stone. He tried to decipher the Spanish words and it took a while, but he deduced that the church first began construction in the year 1000 B.C. Wow.

The Camino really was an ancient pathway. Outside the church again, he walked toward Cizur Menor on flagstone paths, liking the sound his feet made on them. He found the terrain changing constantly and liked the different sights as smells. Mistletoe seemed to grow everywhere as did a small purple flower that looked like a daisy. He didn't pass a single soul until he reached Cizur Menor.

It was a charming little village, filled with all kinds of

pilgrims strolling a small square that had pretty stone houses with small balconies filled with a proliferation of window boxes. He found the pharmacy. He walked inside and purchased a box of Band-Aids, not that he could really squeeze one more thing in his backpack, but the blister on his heel had begun to throb. He found only one, not two cafes, the second one having closed down. At the first cafe, he snagged a small, vacant table just as another man made a grab for it. He was surprised to see it was Theodore.

They greeted each other. Antonio wasn't sure who was more surprised, but he hardly had time to think about it because the next thing he knew, Zebediah was there, his hand under Antonio's elbow.

"You have a boo-boo?" Zebediah asked. The enticing mixture of the real concern he saw in the other man's eyes plus the cute way he had with words filled the empty, echoing canyons of Antonio's famished soul. His breath caught in his throat and he could only nod.

Theodore said something, but Antonio was lost in Zebediah's green gaze. He found himself sitting down and was surprised how calm he was as he gingerly removed his boot. It was amazing how such a small, silly thing like a heat blister could cause such strife. He started to peel off his socks and began to examine the blister that was now causing a ridiculous amount of agony.

When Theodore spoke again, Antonio looked up, aware of Zebediah kneeling beside him, holding his foot in his hands. He felt a surge of heat that caused sweat to bead out on his forehead and upper lip. Dang. One touch from another man and he was a feverish wreck.

Antonio shivered, surprised when Zebediah rolled his socks back over his foot.

"Coffee?" he asked Antonio who was stunned to find the blister no longer hurt. He felt along the heel in a surreptitious way as he pretended to look over the pilgrim's menu that Zebediah had just handed him. He couldn't feel a Band-Aid or any pain from his blister.

"What looks good to you?" Zebediah asked. Antonio thought he had to be imaging things. Zebediah had just done a good job of putting the Band-Aid on him, that's all. He slipped his boot back on, so grateful the blister no longer ached.

He and Zebediah ordered Spanish omelets and coffee. Theodore had just eaten, and said he'd been about to leave when he spotted Antonio. He said he would stay with them as they ate. The food was wonderful, but then Antonio was so hungry a chipmunk on a stick might have appealed to him. He longed to find out more about Zebediah, beyond the fact that he was smoking hot and had an American accent, but Theodore dominated the conversation. He chattered on about the friends he was supposed to meet and how he couldn't understand what had happened to them. Antonio said little. He had a horrible feeling that Theodore, too, was attracted to Zebediah and would want to walk with them both and Antonio had such a strong desire to be alone with the mysterious Zebediah.

He was surprised when Theodore paid for all three meals and suggested they walk together. To Antonio's disappointment, Zebediah seemed keen on the idea. They began to walk, passing several ancient monuments Antonio might have missed had Theodore not pointed them out. He'd spotted the famous windmills in the distance leading to Puente la Reina and was excited to see them up close.

Theodore however pointed to their left. "Look over at this old water fountain," he said. "There's a wonderful old legend attached to it. Oh, look, there's water in it." They all veered off the now-rocky path and Theodore plunged into his story.

"It seems there was an ancient pilgrim who was so thirsty he was on the point of death when another traveler appeared out of nowhere and showed him this fountain. Before he would let the pilgrim drink, the traveler revealed himself as the devil. He would only allow the pilgrim to take a drink if he renounced Jesus, God and the Virgin Mary."

"What did he do?" Antonio asked.

"He refused to renounce them and almost died, but then another traveler appeared just in time, only this one was Saint James in disguise. He helped the traveler drink his water. I can't help thinking how much more interesting this story would have been had the pilgrim denounced Jesus. How about you, Antonio, would you renounce him?"

Antonio just stared at him. Theodore had to be insane. Yes, only a crazy man would ask him a question like this.

"Of course not," he said. He turned his back on Theodore and made his way back down to the trail again. Zebediah and Theodore caught up with him. Antonio was upset with Theodore, wondering why he would ask Antonio such an obviously vile thing.

"I think you hurt Antonio's feelings," Zebediah suddenly said. "You should apologize, I think."

Antonio was shocked. It surprised him that Zebediah could be so sensitive.

"Oh, come on," Theodore said. "It was a joke. We're both in similar situations, only I'm slightly ahead of the curve."

Zebediah shot a glance in Antonio's direction. "How so?" he asked.

"We're both men of the cloth, we're both questioning . . . well, I'd say that judging by the way you two keep looking at each other that he's gay. Again, I'm ahead of him here because I've actually had sex with a man."

"You have?" Antonio asked, forgetting all about being mad at Theodore. "Who? When?" He couldn't believe what he was hearing. Theodore had been a virgin the last time they'd spoken which was the night before.

"Last night." Theodore had a huge grin on his face. As soon as you fell asleep in the *albergue,* this strange man came in. Man, he was hot. He had kinda funky breath, but his name was Matthias. He was European and —"

"Oh, my God," Zebediah said, interrupting.

"Yeah." Theodore rocked on his heels. "I said that a lot last night. That man was really something." He glanced at Antonio. "I think you two ought to go for it."

Antonio was mortified. He didn't know what to say. It didn't help that when he glanced at Zebediah, the man looked horrified at the prospect.

CHAPTER THREE

From the moment Zeb had met Theodore on the way to Cizur Menor, he had sensed something off about him. He had a handsome face and cut a fine figure with his slim but muscular build and short, cropped brown hair but he was uncomfortable to be around. He seemed ditzy and couldn't complete a sentence, yet he would *not* stop talking. Zeb had been so consumed with his own problems he hadn't really given the matter much thought until he'd encountered Theodore a second time at the cafe and wouldn't leave him and Antonio alone. His attraction to Antonio was strong. His appeal was immediate with his sexy blue eyes and blond hair, but the man had known the darkness.

Zeb had delved into Antonio's psyche immediately and saw his naked need. He saw the trainee priest's most secret fantasies and it appealed to Zeb enormously. There was so much loss in Antonio that Zeb felt protective of him. It wasn't just that he really wanted to fuck the guy — which he did — but that there was something vulnerable about him. Now he knew what it was.

When Theodore descended on them, Zeb focused on him trying to figure out if his nutty behavior was a sign of mental instability or demonic possession.

Matthias had materialized in person and fucked him.

That meant that the demon master was here, keeping an eye on Zeb, and if he sensed any attraction between Zeb and Antonio, he could easily invade him. Zeb couldn't live with that. He needed to contact Raph. And soon. Raph would know what to do.

Zeb's mind raced. When he'd landed in Pomplona right on Dead Man's Lane, he hadn't known which of his supernatural abilities he still had left. He found two. He could read minds and he still had his healing powers. Matthias hadn't been able to delete those. Not that he could touch Zeb's healing powers since they had been his before his problems with the devil began. In fact, they were the reason *why* he had these problems in the first place.

He had seen how hurt Antonio was when Theodore made the crack about denouncing God. Matthias had been unable to complete his possession of the young Franciscan monk because Theodore's faith in God was so strong. A few more nights of scorching sex however, and Theodore would be in Matthias's powerful grip.

All three men grew quiet as they began the arduous climb, the worst climb they would face that day according to know-it-all Theodore. Suddenly, Zeb felt terrible for feeling so negative about Theodore. He knew he was a good man underneath it all, struggling with a powerful force he had no way of controlling.

Theodore breathed heavily as they climbed the hill that would bring them to a series of crop fields. He grabbed Antonio's arm as they walked toward the windmills and the metal sculptures on the side of the road.

"Sorry," he said. "I feel faint. I have no idea what's wrong with me."

Zeb knew exactly what was wrong with him. Matthias had vacated his attempts to possess him. There must have been trouble in hell. Too bad for Theodore. By nightfall, Matthias would return in order to complete his conquest.

"Let's rest a while," Zeb said, his tone more terse than he intended. He felt a real concern for Theodore, but sensed Antonio's increasing withdrawal.

He thinks I don't like him. Damn.

Theodore misinterpreted Zeb's tone. "Please," he said, "Don't worry about me. You too go ahead."

Zeb shook his head. "No way. We're in this together." He needed to protect Theodore. He could take care of both him and Antonio. Once he secured Raph's help, Theodore would be safe.

One more ridge and they were over the worst of the walk. Zeb and Antonio each held Theodore up, an arm on either side of him as they entered the town of Alto del Perdon.

On the side of the road between cast iron sculptures of ancient pilgrims on horseback, two donkeys and even a dog, stood a man at a small kiosk. He was British and was cracking jokes with a group of tourists sprawled on the ground beside him. The man sold ice-cold cans of soda, medicinal supplies and he had free cups of tea.

A few of the men and women in the first group were treating the blisters on their feet.

"Everybody gets them," the kiosk owner said. "Hazard of the walk. You want a cup of tea, mate?"

Antonio and Zeb each took a cup. Antonio bought Theodore a can of soda. Theodore downed it quickly and began to doze against a tree.

"We need to get him inside a church," Zeb said in low tones to Antonio.

Antonio looked startled. "Really? Why?"

"I can't explain right now."

Antonio's gaze darted from left to right. "Okay."

"I can explain later. We just need to get him inside a church."

Antonio gave him a long look, then pulled out a dog-eared guidebook from his backpack. "There's a church in Eunate, about six and a half miles from here. It's a twelfth century church a little off the beaten track but that's the closest one."

"It's off the beaten track you say?"

"Yes. It's on a road called Monreal Las Campanas which we take once we reach The Camino town of Obanos. Eunate is three miles off The Camino way. So, like I said, we're looking at a six-mile walk from here." Antonio turned a page. "Hey, this is weird, for some reason this is the point where a lot of pilgrims died in the past and this church is where a lot of them are buried."

"Good. Very good." Zeb liked the sound of this. The little church sounded better and better. He just had to hope he could contact Raph there. He smiled to himself. Raph would adore the idea of all those dead pilgrims.

"Why are you smiling? Antonio asked, his brow furrowing.

"I was just thinking how far we've come as a race . . . and yet, not so far, really. Okay, help me up with our friend here."

They raised Theodore up and he opened his eyes. Zeb didn't like what he was seeing. Man, Matthias must have done a number on this guy. Theodore was almost completely lost to himself. Had they been back in civilization when he'd been psychically attacked, people would have said he'd had a psychotic break.

Theodore needed to walk. They needed to keep him moving. Zeb urged him forward and Antonio bought three cans of soda.

"I'm okay," Theodore said, sounding as weak as a kitten. The three men walked past the first town of Maruzabal and Zeb noticed Theodore seemed better. He'd lost the vacant look in his eyes and he wasn't jabbering on like a loon. In another mile they would arrive in the town of Obanos.

The last mile sped by quickly. Obanos was a lively town with food and accommodations.

"I don't know about you, but I want a meal. I think Theodore needs it too," Antonio said. "If we're going to detour to

Eunate, it's still a mile and a half from here and once we get there, I don't think there's food or accommodations."

Zeb thought fast. It was late afternoon. They were on the cusp of the next Camino stage, the town of Puente la Reina, but they couldn't go there. They needed to hole up in Eunate for the night.

"We could sleep in the church," Antonio said. "We'd be safe there."

Safe. Zeb's head began to spin. The guys in hell would laugh about that one.

"Okay," he said aloud. "Let's make it quick, though."

Antonio seemed to have his heart set on some restaurant called Casa Pepe. It wasn't marked and it took a lot of asking around before they found it. It was a hole and corner type place with cream color stone walls and rustic wooden benches, but it was the best meal Zeb could remember having as a human being.

Theodore was much perkier, and Antonio was all smiles as the couple who ran the restaurant brought them hearty, rustic bread in baskets, refilling them constantly. They each ordered a glass of wine and then the wife brought a huge terracotta platter to the table with the local delicacy. It was a pork noodle casserole that made Zeb's soul sing with happiness. He loved the seasoning of paprika, fresh parsley and manchega cheese. They scraped the platter clean with their forks.

Zeb was so unhappy when they finished their meal. He caught Antonio's gaze and saw the same look of woe on his face. They all laughed.

"Excuse me," Zeb said. He left the table for just a moment, rushing around the back of the restaurant into an alleyway.

"Raph," he said aloud. "I summon you to help a child of God. You must come before sunset to the church of Eunate." He paused. "I know I already owe you one, but this is important." He paused again when he heard footsteps. They receded again and he whispered this time, "*Auxiliis indiget monachus*, A monk needs help," then ran back inside again.

He heard a crack of thunder outside. Raph was still the same old showoff.

Everybody in the restaurant talked about the sound of thunder. It would have been so easy to stay and relax, but Zeb poked the other two.

"Come on," he said. "We have to keep moving." He would have paid for the meal if he had any money, but he'd lost the wallet when he met Antonio. Somebody had grabbed it out of his hands. He now realized it had probably been Matthias.

So far, he'd gotten by on water and food scraps and, thanks to Theodore and Antonio, two good meals in one day. He watched Antonio putting money down for their meals. Zeb thanked him.

"My treat next time," he said, wondering how on earth he'd pull off a feat like that.

"Why do we have to go to this church anyway?" Theodore asked. He sounded a little whiny. Now that he was under Watcher protection and also had Antonio on his side, his personality was coming back. "I want to get on the way to Puente la Reina. Maybe my friends are there. Maybe . . ." his voice dropped and his cheeks colored, "that Matthias guy will be there."

Zeb hated to interfere with Theodore's mental clarity, but he couldn't have the man muttering Matthias's name aloud. Just saying a demon's name could bring him to you.

"You'll see," Zeb said, enigmatically. He coughed right in Theodore's ear, sending a mental cloud of white noise into his brain. Theodore shook his head.

"Sorry." Zeb grabbed his elbow. They moved along the road to their left and proceeded in the late afternoon warmth along the gentle, country walk.

"I must say this is more pleasant than the walk to the Alto,"

Antonio said.

"Really?" Theodore asked, his head tilted at him at an odd angle. "I don't remember any of it. I seem to be in a kind of . . . fog."

Zeb had to stop himself from laughing. Antonio kept up an amusing line of chatter about his first night's stay on The Camino and how he hadn't expected there to be no sheets on the bed.

"I don't think they'd get away with that in the States," he said. "The maids' union would be all over them."

"Was it so awful?" Zeb asked.

"No. It was a reminder that we're not here for a spa vacation. It's a pilgrimage."

Zeb sensed they were heading into dangerous territory. He didn't sense Matthias around them . . . yet, but he didn't want to engage in any negative conversation that could give the ancient demon the idea that both Antonio and Theodore were ripe for the picking.

He swiftly changed the subject. "How did you get the name Antonio when you're so blond and fair?" he asked.

Antonio laughed. "My mother always liked the name. She married my father at the height of her career and chose him over an Italian photographer she was dating. She said calling me by his name was a kind of homage to him."

James gaped at him. "And your father didn't mind?"

Antonio laughed again. "My father is so crazy about my mother he would take her if she wanted to bring circus elephants into the house."

"She's a . . . model?" Zeb had already read this in Antonio's mind but wanted to be careful not to alarm the guy.

"Yes, she was. A very successful one. Summer Rain was her name. She still works a little."

"I've seen her. Oh, wow." James snapped his fingers. "You have her hair."

Antonio shrugged. "Yeah."

They reached the church at last. They were about an hour away from sunset.

"Should we go in?" Antonio asked.

They all stepped forward. Zeb had no idea what to expect. As a full-fledged storm demon, he would never have attempted it. The church doors would have shut themselves on his cloven hoofs. As a Watcher, it was still dicey. He watched the other two go inside and then he heard a voice.

"Dude."

He turned. They all turned, Antonio and Theodore hovering in the doorway.

"Go inside," Zeb said. "I'll be right with you."

They obeyed and he heaved a small side of relief.

"Dude," said the voice again. It came from a huge tabby cat lying on one of the stone tombs in the graveyard.

"Raph?"

The cat yawned, meowed, then said, "At your service."

Zeb sat beside him. "Couldn't you find a human body?"

"At this short notice? You're lucky I showed up here at all. You still owe me."

"Yeah, I know."

"The problem with helping somebody in trouble is that they remember it the next time they're in trouble."

Zeb grinned. "I'll owe you plenty."

"Yeah, you will. So what do you want me to do with your pilgrim, exactly?"

Zeb paused. He hadn't expected his first conversation with Raph in almost a hundred years to go like this. He'd expected to feel emotional. Well, he did, sort of, but the demonic side of him had tamped out some of his finer qualities.

"Raph, I want you to protect him, take him over. Get him out of here."

The cat went silent, stretching out, then extending his paw, began to wash his face.

"Matthias could pick somebody else you know," Raph said between licks. His voice still had the deep, lilting resonance he'd remembered. As a child growing up in the Catskills, Raph had spoken to him. Usually at night. The visits scared him at first. It was weird that he suddenly thought about this now

"It's true that Matthias could pick on another innocent, but I plan on sticking by Antonio and keeping away anyone else who plans to get close to him."

"Why me?" the cat asked. Typical Raph, always fishing for compliments.

Zeb rolled his mental eyes. "You're my favorite angel, Raphael. The biggest, the best, the bad-ass sexiest Archangel ever. Who else would I ask?"

"You forgot best looking."

"That, too."

"I'll do it. But you know we need to stay here tonight. Your hot-hoofed buddy will probably be waiting in Puente la Reina."

"Yeah, I know."

"Your friend Theodore's acquired a taste for cock. I don't know that I can dissuade him from wanting to go get some."

"Then introduce him to the magic of self-gratification."

The cat actually pouted. "You're no fun."

Why did Raph like to challenge him all the time?

"Zeb, I don't think your boyfriend's gonna like spending the night here. This old church is kinda creepy."

"We'll be with him." *Why does the idea of Antonio being my boyfriend make me feel like a happy teenager?*

"You'll have to keep his mouth full, so he doesn't have time to complain."

Zeb looked at the cat. "For an angel, you have the dirtiest mind. And the filthiest mouth."

"I know. That's why I'm your favorite." The cat meowed

again. "I'm only helping you because of what you did for the kids in Michigan."

"They're okay, aren't they?"

"Yes, but it was a close call. The little boy . . . he got spanked by his mother for not keeping a closer eye on his sister."

Zeb found his teeth grinding at the thought. The mother was an ass. He shook his head.

"She had to take her frustrations out on somebody. Hey, your friends are coming. How long am I supposed to stay inside Theodore?"

"Until you can convince him to return home. Just please, see him safely back to Baltimore."

"Dude," the cat said again, his tone reproachful.

"Are you coming in?" Antonio asked.

Zeb got to his feet and nodded. He smiled down at the cat, bent and stroked its head. The cat preened for a moment, then got up and padded over to Theodore who looked down at it.

"Let's have a look around," Zeb told Antonio. He took his arm and steered him away.

"Will he be okay?" Antonio asked. "He's acting so freaking weird."

"Yeah, I know."

"What's going on? Why all the mystery? Why did we come here? Why —"

They rounded the corner and Zeb pushed Antonio up against the old stone wall of the church. He felt Antonio's breath on his lips, hardly able to wait for the moment their mouths met.

Antonio inhaled sharply as Zeb claimed his mouth. Their kiss was sweet, innocent at first. He could taste the surprise in Antonio's hesitant kisses. Antonio moved his mouth open as Zeb slipped his tongue between his lips. Zeb found it charming that the man had no idea how to kiss.

A virgin.

Thank the Lord. That meant that he could easily enter the church as long as he was in the company of a male virgin.

"Come on," he said, taking his mouth from Antonio."

Antonio looked dizzy. "What? Why? Did I do something wrong?"

Zeb put his hands on Antonio's face. "You did nothing wrong and I swear the next time I kiss you I won't stop until you tell me to, but we need to get inside now."

"But—"

Zeb could hear the distant sound of thunder. Matthias was coming. *Shit.* In the far distance, he could hear the flap of wings. Matthias was moving faster.

"Ready?" Theodore asked. The cat was walking out of the graveyard now, so Zeb knew that Raph had moved inside him. The flapping sound grew louder. *Double Shit.* Matthias was maybe a minute away.

Raph sprinted up the few stone steps into the church. Zeb held Antonio's hand in his and led him inside. He felt a frisson of electrical current pass through him.

"Ow!" Antonio said, pulling his hand away.

"Sorry." Zeb bolted the church door closed. Outside the wind that had started began to whip at the walls and windows of the church.

Zeb looked for the Holy Water font and found it. Theodore stood before him.

"You need to bless all three of us with Holy Water," Zeb told Antonio.

"But—"

"Quickly now."

The doors and windows began to rattle. Antonio looked frightened. He glanced at Theodore who just smiled.

"What's going on?" Antonio dipped his fingers in the water, but hesitated.

"Hurry," Zeb said, trying to scream.

Antonio anointed Theodore, then Zeb, then himself. The wind eased down but then the dim lights that had been on in the church went black.

"He's trying to get in," Theodore suddenly said, except it was Raph's voice.

"What—" Antonio looked confused.

"The relic. The sacred relic. Every church has one. Find it," Theodore/Raph said, and ran to the side of the church.

Damn. Zeb had no idea where to start looking for a sacred relic.

"It would be in the sanctuary, but I doubt it's just sitting there," Antonio said. "It's most probably buried."

"Let's try." Antonio charged along the aisle, passing the cute rows of pews and passed from the nave to the transept. Electricity shot through him.

"Antonio?"

He turned. Antonio hadn't come with him. He stood back in the nave, watching him.

"What's going on?" he asked, his words careful and distinct.

"I'm trying to prevent your friend from being taken over by demonic possession."

Antonio opened and closed his mouth, then blinked. Zeb felt the sweat trickling down his back and under his armpits. He kept getting zapped. Unless Antonio came with him, the electric shocks would continue.

"Please," he muttered, each word sheer torture now. He held out his hand.

Antonio came toward him.

"What kind of creature are you?" he asked.

"I'm a Watcher."

Antonio stopped on the second of three steps leading to the transept.

"A Watcher? Such things exist?" Antonio looked at him in wonderment.

He thinks that's exciting? Wait until I tell him I'm also . . .probably still a storm demon.

Antonio joined him in the transept and the shocks stopped. Outside the wind stopped howling.

Theodore had crept along the far left aisle and joined them on the transept.

"The relic is probably buried under the tombstone there." Theodore pointed.

He was right. There was an ancient tombstone in the transept, built into the floor it had a stone marker and some words in Spanish, but how in the world could they dig it up.

"We might be okay," Theodore said suddenly. "The wind's died down."

Outside, Zeb heard howling. Yeah. They were safe. For now.

"So, we can't tear up the church looking for this . . .relic, what next?" Zeb asked.

"Holy wine."

Zeb repeated this under his breath.

The three men walked into the sanctuary, the private domain of the church. Theodore walked over to the altar, which bore a red cloth, a golden goblet covered in more red fabric and a gilt box that stood between two tapers.

"Could the relic be in here?" Theodore asked. "Many churches keep their relics between tapers and bound in gold."

Zeb's head began to hurt. He realized that Raph was trying to tell him this, while still trying to sound like Theodore.

Somebody was pounding the front door of the church. Zeb blinked. Matthias and whoever he'd brought with him could get in any second now. He heard footsteps outside.

"You open it," Zeb said.

Antonio said nothing. He looked completely freaked out.

"*You* open it," Theodore countered. "Protection has to be

40

given, remember?"

No, Zeb hadn't remembered. It had been decades since his last human steps on Earth and a lot of good things he remembered had been tortured from his mind in his early days of residing in hell. If he ever had to go back, he didn't know how he was going to survive it.

"I'll do it," Antonio said. "Zeb, why are you shaking?"

"He's remembering some things," Theodore said. "Very bad things."

Antonio put a hand on Zeb's arm. "Have you two met before?"

"You could say that." Zeb's whole body felt like it was about to explode. Sweat dripped from his face.

"I won't let anyone hurt you." Theodore's voice was strong.

Zeb looked at him, the pain in his body and heart too much to bear. Being this close to the altar was like holding his hands in fire.

"I'll do it." Antonio picked up the gilt box but couldn't find the opening.

"Press the stone in the middle," Theodore said.

Antonio glanced at him, put the box on the altar and pressed. The box slid open, a drawer lined in red velvet sliding out from the base.

They all stared. It was a series of bones.

"It's a humerus," Theodore said. His voice was not his own. It was Raph speaking. "*Virtus and daemones*. This is a gift. Quick, Zeb. Touch it. It's the shoulder bone of Saint Nicholas. Renounce your deal with the devil."

"Your what?" Antonio barked.

"I renou —"

The front door smashed open, the wind whipping down the aisle. Leaves, pebbles, twigs and dirt flew through the church.

"Take it," Zeb yelled at Theodore, thrusting the gilt box into his hands. He fumbled with the closure locks. "Take it. Take it and protect him. I'll take care of Antonio."

Theodore ran out of the sanctuary. He must have found the exit. Zeb moved Antonio behind him then pushed him towards the side door.

"No!"

Zeb stopped. The voice he heard was outside the church. The wind had died down. Zeb closed his eyes. Theodore was okay, but he knew the demons were after him. He had to be here with Antonio waiting for when they returned.

"We need to wait," he told Antonio who had one hand on the door.

"I—I don't want to."

"It's safest here. They can make a lot of noise, but they can't come in."

"Are you sure? What about Theodore? Will he be okay?"

Zeb nodded. He kept the side door unlatched for Theodore, hoping there was enough of his old connected with Raph for him to read his thoughts that they were hiding in the sanctuary, waiting for him.

"Who are you?" Antonio asked.

"I already told you. My name is Zebediah."

"Yes . . . but you said you're a Watcher. I want to know what's going on. I want to know how you healed my blister, how you appear to read my mind . . . and what the devil is going on with Theodore."

"You said it right there. The devil is going on with Theodore."

Zebediah walked out of the sanctuary toward the front door. There was a lot of debris on the ground and a couple of vases of wildflowers had been toppled in the wind, but the church was otherwise okay. He locked the front door again, this time throwing the heavy wooden bolt across it. It didn't appear to have been locked in a long time and he almost gave up until Antonio helped him with it.

A couple of windows had blown open. He closed and bolted them. He began lighting candles around the church.

"I'm waiting," Antonio said, following him around the nave. "Give me one good reason why I shouldn't run right out of here."

"Because, I can't protect you out there."

Zeb frowned. He couldn't remember what kind of prayers his father had said as he'd lit candles in their church. He just had to hope everything he was doing would work.

The back door opened, and Theodore returned.

"I lost them," he said, only it was Raph talking, not Theodore.

"How come his voice changed?" Antonio asked.

Zeb looked at him. "If I tell you what you want to know, you have to promise not to leave here. I understand you're frightened . . ."

"Just tell me."

"Is that a promise?"

"No promises. I'm surprised I'm still standing here."

Zeb licked his lips, suddenly terribly thirsty.

"A long, long time ago, my father abused certain . . . abilities I had. He used them for gain and profit. The devil came after him. It's a long story but basically my father sold his soul to the devil."

"Is this a joke?" Antonio stared at him.

"No. Does it sound like I'm joking?" Zeb felt wretched. He looked at Raph. "I'm not explaining this very well."

"I think you're doing a good job." He sat in one of the pews, opened up Theodore's backpack and pulled out an apple. He began to eat it.

"You're the most disobedient angel I ever met," Zeb grumbled.

"I'm not disobedient. I came as soon as you called me."

"Angel?" Antonio sounded weak.

"Archangel, actually. Archangel Raphael." Zeb watched Antonio's facial expression freeze. "I've known him since I was a child. He came to me when I first realized I had the power to heal. He always helped me."

"You were a handsome, sweet boy," Raph said, chomping his apple.

"My father took advantage of me . . . but I couldn't see him go to hell. As far as I was concerned, my father was a minister . . . a good and kind man who helped a lot of people. We were poor. People started giving us money and it went to his head. It spoiled him. As far as I was concerned my gift was his curse. When the devil gave me the choice of going to hell in his place, I took it."

"Why?" Antonio shrieked. "Who would do that? I can't believe any of this." He began to pace. "I just wanted to go for a walk. I wanted answers . . . not more problems."

"You know," Raph said, sitting up, "You might be right. You may not be explaining things very well."

He got up, handed Zeb his half-eaten apple and stood in front of Antonio, putting his hands on his shoulders.

"Zeb was recently tossed out of hell. He was a storm demon, but not a very good one. He was given a second chance as a Watcher, but a Watcher isn't supposed to intervene."

"Lemme guess, he did."

"He saved a little girl from being taken by a pedophile."

Antonio said nothing.

Zeb picked up the story again. "I was thrown out yesterday morning and found myself landing in the Running of the Bulls. I met you. I have a chief nemesis in . . . hell . . . his name is Matthias and—"

Antonio's face went white. "Isn't that the name of the man who seduced Theodore?"

Zeb nodded. "Exactly. I realized straight away that Matthias was here and trying to possess Theodore."

Antonio's face registered comprehension. "So that's why we came here. For protection." Before Zeb could respond, Antonio asked, "What is a storm demon?"

Zeb felt himself involuntarily shiver. "We are creatures banished to dark, desolate places. We cause storms, we . . ." he paused, "we are destined to live alone."

"He's not telling you everything." Raph put his hand on Zeb's shoulder. "He kept rescuing travelers on the road, so they put him in the desert. He saved a couple in a car . . . and a camel."

Antonio was staring at Theodore now, because Raph's real face had started to emerge and the beautiful, dark-haired angel who had been Zeb's only friend when his father had isolated him, virtually imprisoned him . . . Raph was here.

Zeb felt tears pricking the back of his eyes. He understood now why he hadn't been affected when he first started talking to Raph outside the church. He'd hidden himself in a cat.

"I have missed you," Raph said, his hand squeezing Zeb's shoulder.

Zeb fought his roiling emotions.

"You're the . . . you're *the* Archangel Raphael?" Antonio's voice dropped in awe.

Raph smiled. Light filled the church. Zeb and Antonio could only stare at Raph's magnificence. The angel shimmered out of view again and Theodore looked like himself.

"And virtues and daemons?" Antonio asked.

Zeb looked at him. "Virtues and evils . . . I was about to renounce my ties to the devil when his apprentice made his appearance."

Antonio threw up his hands. "This is too much. I can't take it all in. The devil is tempting me. That's why this is happening to me. I can't stay here. I have to go."

"Please don't leave." Zeb felt wretched. He had no power to stop the man he genuinely cared about, but he also couldn't leave him out in the open, vulnerable to a psychic attack.

"Save it. Please. This is just . . . more than I can handle. I'm having a life crisis. I can't handle my own and yours, too."

"Go with him," Zeb said. Theodore looked at him. "You're vulnerable if we leave you alone."

"Better me than him."

Raph shook his head, letting Zeb see his beautiful face again.

"You never learn, my friend."

Zeb opened his mouth, but Antonio ran up to the transept without looking back. He knocked over a huge gold cross and ran through the sanctuary.

"I'll catch up with him." The Angel handed him the gilt box containing the relic. "Open it, I will hear your confession."

A storm started raging outside.

"Go to him, please."

"In a minute."

Zeb didn't argue. He pressed open the box again and the drawer opened. He put his right hand on the relic of Saint Nicholas and said, "I renounce my allegiance to the devil. I ask for God's pardon."

The storm stopped.

"Is that a good or bad sign?" he asked Raph.

"Keep going."

"I am a child of God, a student of day. A son of the light."

Zeb felt the pain starting in his left foot and shooting up his body."

"I am a child of the light, not of the night," he said, panting now.

"Very good." Raph pushed him toward a pew. "Hold this and lie down until the pain subsides. You will experience a new kind of hell, but you'll get through it."

He put a cool hand on Zeb's forehead, but Zeb was already in hell.

"I am so sorry." Raph's voice cracked and the great angel's tear fell on Zeb's forehead. "Both times you needed me I have been unable to help. Give me the word and I will stay here."

"No. Antonio needs you more."

Raph nodded. "You, the great healer . . . nobody is here when you need it yourself."

Zeb heard the devil himself calling him and his eyes closed. So hard to resist. But resist he must. He kept saying over and over again, "I am a child of God, a student of day. A son of the light."

He heard a wild cackling above him . . . oh no. He looked up into the face of Matthias. How had he gotten in? What could have gone wrong?

CHAPTER FOUR

Antonio hadn't walked far when Theodore caught up with him. It had been a strange, unpleasant feeling walking in total darkness. His backpack suddenly felt much lighter with the big galoot standing next to him.

"Is it you or the angel?"

"We are both here."

"Yeah, right. Whatever."

"You saw my face. You know I'm real."

"I guess. I don't want to talk about this right now. I need to think."

"No problem. I can be quiet."

"That would make a nice change."

"That's not very nice."

"I thought you said you were going to be quiet."

"No. I said I *can* be quiet. There's a big difference."

Antonio frowned. "If you're an angel, how come you're so irritating?"

"Ah. Well, that's because I'm in a human body and humans are not perfect." Raph went quiet all of a sudden. "You know what? It's so nice to have a penis again." He glanced at Antonio. "Don't you want to use it all the time? I mean, I want to. I want to pee constantly just so I can fondle it."

Antonio stared at him. In spite of everything, Theodore/Raph made him laugh.

"I actually dream about using it for other things."

Theodore/Raph seemed to be weighing his response. "That's completely natural."

"Have you been inside a human body before?"

Theodore/Raph smiled. "Not for a long time. I used to help Zeb in his healings."

"Right, you're the angel of healing."

They walked in silence for a while. "I was in a man's body a while ago. He hovered between life and death. His family prayed to me. He was a good man. I was happy to help."

"Ever been in a woman's body?"

Theodore/Raph smiled then. "More often than not. I was in the body of a young computer technician who went to Afghanistan to teach the women how to use computers. You probably know women there are forbidden to learn, forbidden to work. Rachel was part of a network of people who helped the war widows learn new trades. These women usually starve to death because in their country when their husbands pass, they are not allowed to live with their fathers . . . they are not allowed to work."

"What happened to Rachel?" Antonio didn't think he wanted to know but he had to ask.

"She was killed in a bomb explosion. She was escorted every day by bodyguards to her classes. The bomb went off. I was sent to help. She lingered for a few days." He paused. "She was a sweet girl. Sometimes . . ."

His voice cut off and he picked up his pace. Antonio scrambled to keep up with him.

"Sometimes what?"

"I'll put it this way. I understand why Zebediah intervenes. He sees the future and wants to help. You've never seen anything like the power he has in his hands."

"Oh, yes, I have. He healed my foot blister."

"That's nothing. I've seen him make crippled children walk. His loss was . . . keenly felt on this plane."

"Why did he make such a pact with the devil?" Antonio couldn't understand this. Night fell deeper and he was relieved when he saw lights up ahead for the town of Obanos. He liked the idea of staying there for the night. There were no hostels that he could recall from his research and it was too dark to read his guidebook now, but there were, he remembered, rooms for rent. Maybe he'd even get sheets on the bed! His mind came over all dreamy at the notion of crisp, clean white sheets, a big fluffy towel . . .

"He did it for selfless reasons. That's all I can tell you. I can't say much more than that. It's his tale to tell."

Theodore/Raph's face looked pained. Antonio could see even in the darkness that the angel cared about Zeb.

"He stayed back at the church. Why?"

Theodore/Raph adjusted his backpack on his shoulders. "Zeb renounced his allegiance to er . . . you-know-who. He is better off there as he goes through his penance."

"Penance?"

"You don't want to know."

"You're right." Antonio nodded emphatically. "I sure don't." He looked forward to a glass of wine, a good night's rest and another day of walking. He didn't want to think about angels and demons, good versus evil. Why did he care if the storm demon went through a penance?

They reached the town and began to knock on doors together.

"We should share a room," Theodore/Raph said.

"Look—"

"It's for your own protection. Tomorrow, in daylight, all of this will seem much better."

"Will it?" Antonio couldn't stop the bitterness from seeping into his tone.

They followed the little old lady who owned the rooms for rent, and she gestured to two small beds made up with sheets and blankets. A big pillow sat at the head of each one.

"Perfect." Antonio opened up his wallet.

"I've got this," Raph said. "Teddy's a rich boy. Trust fund kid. I know you worked hard for every dime you've saved."

"How do you—never mind." Antonio sat on the first bed, dropped his backpack on the floor, undid his boots and lay back on the bed.

The old lady said something in Spanish.

"She wants to bring us tea and cakes," Theodore/Raph reported.

Antonio ran a hand across his tired eyes. "I wouldn't say no. As a matter of fact, it's a good think she doesn't speak English because I might ask her to marry me."

Theodore/Raph grinned. "You must like tea and cakes a lot."

"I like any nice gesture." Antonio turned to his side, watching Theodore drop his load and removed his boots. Antonio grinned as he watched the other man peeling off his damn socks and wiggling his feet.

"Aahhh." His hand flew to his crotch. Antonio couldn't help laughing. "You should wait. Tea and cakes, remember?"

"I think you have a few issues around food," Theodore said.

There was a knock at the door, which had only been ajar. The old lady shuffled in with two glasses of tea stuffed with herbs and thick slices of what looked like pound cake.

Both men sat on their beds. She stood between the beds, finally placing her tray on a chair at the foot of Theodore's bed.

"*Una buena alimentación,*" she said. Antonio already knew this meant, good eating.

She wished them a good night and closed the door behind her.

"Bet she comes back," Theodore muttered. Sure enough, the door popped open again. Antonio had to smile when he saw the enormous plate of fruit she brought with her.

Antonio fumbled in his pockets for change. She was so sweet and humble, thanking him as she backed out of the room again, closing the door behind her.

Raph reached for a grape, popped it into his mouth and frowned.

"I have been in this human body too long. I am already becoming so distrustful."

They ate quietly, listening to the sounds of the small town outside their shared window. Antonio kept running things around in his mind, not liking any of the things that came to him. He had so many questions yet was afraid to ask. The more he knew, the more he was certain that life was just one big unpleasant mystery after another.

More than anything, he worried about Zeb. He cursed his own soft nature. Why should he care about a fallen storm demon?

He felt alternately angry, then sad and finally looked up from the slices of apples in his hands to find Raphael's gaze on him. For it was Raphael. It was the second time he'd seen the Archangel fully and his beauty tore at Antonio's heart.

"Demons are a misunderstood lot," Raphael said to him. "Watchers are the most misunderstood of all. Don't judge him too harshly. He made a decision in the name of love. I know few men who could be so brave."

"If you say so."

"I think you will find so too, when he tells you the truth."

"What makes you think I'll see him again?"

"You've been dreaming of him for months, haven't you?" Antonio almost fell off the bed.

"Whether you realize it or not, you called out to him."

"You know about my dreams?"

"Sure I do. I'm an angel. I know everything."

"Oh, God." Antonio lay back on the bed and put his arm across his face. Suddenly, the light was too bright in the room.

"He has no idea, I'm sure that your soul reached out to him. Remember, he is by nature a healer, not a sexual being."

Antonio didn't know how to interpret this. "What are you saying?" He kept his arm across his eyes. He couldn't look at the Archangel Raphael and talk about sex for heaven's sake.

"I'm just saying his first concern, beyond an attraction to you was protecting you." Raphael pointed a finger back toward himself. "And to me."

"You, or Theodore?"

"Theodore. He's still here. I'm gonna go bathe and play with his wonderful penis."

Antonio couldn't help laughing. Raphael was incorrigible.

He lay on his bed, tried to feel better about things but found himself more and more disturbed. True, the day had been fascinating and . . . he tried not to think about Zeb's handsome face.

When Raphael returned, he gave Antonio a giddy thumbs up. In the bathroom, he quickly bathed and brushed his teeth. Antonio had never felt so tired. He couldn't think. Didn't want to think.

When he returned to the room, he picked up the tray and empty fruit bowl and left them outside the room again. He returned to find Theodore sitting on the edge of his bed, watching him.

"I'm going to leave in the morning, heading back to Paris."

"What?" Antonio was shocked.

"It is Zebediah's wish and I think he's right. Theodore is very vulnerable. I don't think you-know-who will try to target him again, or you. But Theodore needs to go home and deal with his sexuality and his future."

Raphael smiled at him. "And you, you need to keep walking. Your faith is very strong. Besides, I'm sure Zebediah will strike a hard bargain for your freedom."

The hairs stood on the back of Antonio's neck. "Me? Why

would he do that? What does that mean?"

"He will probably give up what few powers he still has so you are left in peace." Raphael gave him a sad smile. "That is why you came here, after all, wasn't it? To find peace."

"What happens to him then?" Antonio couldn't believe what he was hearing.

"Who knows? Only God knows."

"I thought you said you're an angel and you know everything."

Raphael laughed then. "Yes, I did, didn't I?" He lay back on the bed. "I know everything, but I don't say everything. I'll leave it at that."

"How convenient," Antonio muttered. There was silence from the other bed followed by the steady sound of snoring. Yeah, that was super convenient, too.

Matthias leaned over Zeb's crumpled body. Zeb was on the floor of the house in Michigan, the demon master furious that Zeb kept resisting all efforts to renounce his allegiance to the dark lord.

Zeb had no intention of caving in, no matter how much he hurt. He had to remember that in spite of all the physical pain he endured, if he gave in, Antonio and Theodore would be in trouble.

Why do I care about Antonio? He ran out on me. He hates me!

He remembered how it felt to kiss him, such sweet, tentative kisses that could have been so much more. He tried not to think about being naked with Antonio. Oh, that that day would ever come!

"Are you . . . smiling?" Matthias roared.

"I am a child of God, a student of day. A son of the light."

Zeb had had enough. He would keep saying this mantra until Matthias beat him to death. What did he have to live for anyway? His parents were long gone, and love didn't exist in his world.

"Just finish it," he said, as his mouth filled with blood.

"I wish I could, but he's going to want a little more fun. I don't think our lord wants you dead. That would be too easy. Unless you beg forgiveness, he'll send you back to Earth minus your psychic abilities and your power to heal."

"In exchange for leaving Antonio and Theodore alone."

"This has nothing to do with them. This is about you. I want to see you back on Earth fully human with nothing but the clothes on your back. A loser. You always were a loser, Zebediah."

"In exchange for leaving my friends alone." He wanted to add he also never wanted to see Matthias again but that probably went without saying. Matthias had no further interest in a former storm demon, a former Watcher . . . he wanted demons who toed the line and feared him.

"Done." Matthias kicked him in the ear, and he blacked out. When he came to, he was back in the church on the pew. He bled profusely, and his right ear hurt but he was alive. Whether that was a good thing was debatable. He sat up in the pew. What time was it?

He tried to stand but everything hurt. He fell to the ground. He felt the earth move. It must have been midnight. The time of the dead. He heard the whispers of countless ghosts, heard them shuffling toward him. He had fallen between two pews and couldn't move. He was able to turn his head just a little.

What Zebediah saw were ghosts. Many, many ghosts of pilgrims who had all died at The Camino. He felt humbled by their pain, their sorrow for him. He wondered how he could see them all when he'd been stripped of his powers. Ah . . . maybe he was near death . . . just another pilgrim. Maybe they'd come to claim him. He didn't mind . . . except he never thought at the end of time it would be dead strangers touching him.

He'd hope that the last thing he'd be able to look upon was

his mother's face again . . .

Antonio dreamed of the man in the chair again. He closed his eyes and there he was. Watching, waiting. He beckoned Antonio toward him. Antonio couldn't breathe. The man's face was bleeding. He was almost unrecognizable, but he knew it was Zeb.

He crawled to him, but Zeb tried to push him away at the last moment. His head hung down, Antonio beyond frustrated that his hands were bound behind his back. He couldn't touch Zeb's face.

Antonio raised himself up on his knees so that his face touched Zeb's.

He put his forehead to the other man's, Zeb moaning as if that slight contact caused him pain.

Antonio tried to move his lips over Zeb's. Their kisses were wet, but sweet.

"Untie me," Antonio whispered.

"I'm so tired. I am *so* tired."

Antonio awoke in a sweat. He knew something was very wrong with Zebediah. It was difficult to open his eyes, then he realized it was the dead of night. He couldn't see his watch. He fumbled in darkness for the floor beside him.

"What is it?" Theodore asked, his voice sounding sleepy.

"I had a bad dream about Zeb. I—I need to go to him."

Theodore cursed. "I knew this would happen. Come on, let's get going."

They rose from their beds, stood and bumped into each other, fell back on their beds, then Theodore turned on the light.

"I don't suppose you want to wait a couple of hours. We'll need a ride."

Antonio checked his watch. Four-thirty in the morning.

"We can walk . . . I can walk."

"I'm not letting you go alone. We need a car though. If he's injured, we can't handle him alone. We'll have to get him to a hospital."

Antonio was desperate.

Theodore was staring at him. "How did you get blood on your face?" he asked.

Antonio touched his forehead. "I don't know." Then he remembered. The dream. He looked down at his pajama pants and saw his bloodied knees. He looked up and saw the look of horror on Theodore's face.

"Let's go," he said. "Maybe he's okay."

They started throwing on clothes, packing their things again.

"You don't believe that any more than I do," Antonio said. His teeth were chattering, a mixture of fear, surging adrenaline and the chill of the still dark morning.

They left the house, stood outside.

"My feet hurt," Theodore said.

"Mine, too. I've been thinking. He wants you to leave town. You really should. I can go on my own."

"Are you joking? I left that boy alone once already and look where it got me." Theodore shouldered his backpack and stomped off down the road toward the church.

Antonio hardly felt the soreness in his feet once they got moving. It was a shame that the one night he got to sleep on sheets, clean ones at that, he had to get out of bed without enjoying them.

They walked side by side, Antonio realizing he'd left his walking poles back at the house.

"I have to go back and get my poles."

"We'll get them later," Theodore said. "We can't leave him there alone. What if tourists start coming? It'll be daylight soon."

"You're right."

They picked up the pace arriving at the church twenty minutes later. The door was open. They looked at each other and walked inside. The place looked like it had been ransacked.

An old priest came toward them from the sanctuary.

"Hooligans!" he shrieked in rapid fire Spanish to Theodore who translated for Antonio. "There were a dozen of them. I was too afraid to come in here. Then they were gone."

Antonio looked around. He couldn't believe the state of the place.

"They stole the relic," the old priest said. "It's gone."

Antonio stopped between two pews and saw a man's body on the floor wedged beneath one of them.

"Zebediah!" He dropped to his knees, wincing in pain. He touched the prone man's body, but Zeb didn't move. "Theodore, help me!" He turned, but Theodore was gone.

The old priest stood behind him. "Your friend just left. He said to give you this." He handed over a wad of euros.

"Thanks," Antonio muttered. "Can you help my friend?"

Antonio realized he was speaking Spanish to the old man. He must have retained more of the language than he'd realized. The priest hesitated, then came around the other side of the pew. Together they raised Zeb off the floor and onto a pew. His face was a mess, but his eyes opened. He groaned.

"Where's the priest?" he asked in Spanish.

"I'm right here."

"The relic, I have it." He pointed a bloody finger in the direction where he'd been lying.

With a gasp, the priest dropped down, snatched up the box and held it to his chest.

"Guard it well," Zeb said in English. The priest must have understood because he thanked Zeb and took off.

"Are you okay?" Antonio asked Zeb who leaned against him.

"I've been better." he gave him a weak smile. "Did Theodore leave?"

"Yes. He kept his word. He came here with me. Then he vanished. He left us some money."

"Us?"

"Us," Antonio said. "Come on. Can you walk?"

"I can try."

The priest came running in, protesting when he saw Antonio trying to help Zeb out of the pew.

Zeb couldn't stand anyway. The open front door suddenly darkened. Antonio turned and couldn't believe it. The twelve-steppers had just arrived en masse.

"You again," one of them said. "Cripes. What happened to your buddy?"

Zeb seemed to be drifting in and out of consciousness.

"He got attacked by people who tried to ransack the church."

That was sort of true.

"Does he need a hospital? There's a clinic back in Obanos."

"How do we get him there? He can't walk." Antonio fought off exhaustion and panic.

"I'm a doctor," one of the men said. "Let me look at him." he turned to the priest and began talking to him in Spanish.

"He has a horse and cart. We can take him back to Obanos. Now, let's have a look at him."

Antonio stood back and let the doctor examine Zeb. He felt terrible that he'd thought such disparaging things about this group, yet here they were, helping him. They all dived into their First Aid kits to provide bandages, creams, hydrogen peroxide, and then the priest came running. His horse and cart were outside.

It took four men to help Zebediah into the cart, his feet dangling over the edge. Antonio thanked everybody and climbed into the cart with Zeb.

The priest took the reins and they took off back for Obanos.

"Kiss me," Zeb said at one point, looking up at him. Antonio bit his lip then lowered his face. The kiss was so sweet, yet all too brief.

"Are you okay?" Antonio asked, not for the first time.

"I'd be a lot better if you kissed me again."

Antonio stole a glance at the priest who was busy watching the road. Travelers were coming toward them. Antonio bent and kissed Zeb again. They grinned at one another.

At Obanos, the priest made a show of rejecting any money, then happily snatched a few notes.

"Can we go lie down?" Zeb asked. "Where did you stay last night?"

"You can't walk." Antonio was scandalized.

"Yes, I can. This was a spiritual beating. It takes time to heal . . . I need to sleep. Come on, Antonio, help me up."

Antonio was surprised that Zeb was able to take small steps. They walked across the main square to the little house he'd slept in the previous night. The landlady was surprised to see him, then looked amazed at the sight of Zeb.

"Accident?" she asked in English.

"Si, si," Antonio said. He paid for the room for one more night. She'd already made up the beds and brought him his walking poles. Zeb held onto these for support. He fell on the bed Antonio had occupied the night before. Antonio dropped his things on the floor and took the bed beside him. He tried to check his watch, but he was bleary eyed. It looked like eight o'clock but he couldn't be sure.

"Close your eyes," Zeb said. Within seconds they were both fast asleep.

It felt like he'd just closed his eyes and the landlady was back in the room again. Every bone in Zeb's body ached. Behind his eyelids, Matthias was a dim, dark figure, but man, his head hurt. Why did she have to make so much noise? He could hear Antonio talking to her. Then, he opened his eyes and they were both looking down on him.

A flash of Matthias' leer was replaced by the caring concern of the two people standing over him.

"Are you okay?" Antonio looked wretched.

Zeb nodded and shifted a little on the bed.

The landlady spoke to him in Spanish. "I'm calling the doctor. You don't look good."

"I don't have money for a doctor. I'm fine."

"But I have money and you're not fine." Antonio frowned at him.

The landlady said she would be back. Zeb turned to Antonio.

"Kiss me, quick. Before she gets back."

Antonio grinned, hope shining in his eyes. How had Zeb lived without all the things human emotions could bring? He thought back to the house in Michigan. He'd seen the love the small boy had for his sister. He'd given the child back his sense of hope, of trust that the world could be a beautiful place.

Their kiss would have melted a million lit candles. It was smoking hot. They broke off only when they heard the old lady's footsteps.

Zeb smelled coffee and would have kissed her too, had his heart not set itself upon Antonio. He struggled to sit up. The landlady and Antonio helped him, propping pillows behind his back.

He did feel better. It was full daylight outside.

"What time is it?" he asked Antonio.

"Two o'clock in the afternoon." He smiled, pouring a cup of coffee for Zeb. "It's the Spanish way, cafe con leche? I hope you like milk?"

"I love milk." He wrapped his hands around the cup. "What's that on the plate? Are they Magdalenas?"

The old lady cackled and clapped her hands together.

"I've always wanted to try these," Antonio said, handing him one. "I keep seeing these in every town but never managed to eat one yet." They bit into the rich, yet fluffy breakfast cupcakes. He could taste the butter and lemon. The devil could have all his senses if he wanted them, but he thanked God he could see and hear and taste.

"Here have another one."

Antonio passed him a second cake. They ate happily as the landlady opened their rustic striped curtains Zeb had only just realized matched their bed covers. The devil was in the details. The devil. Zeb didn't feel him much.

"Theodore got away okay, didn't he?" he asked Antonio who poured them both more coffee.

"I think so. I haven't been out, but I get that feeling." Antonio's beautiful blue eyes met his. "Don't you?"

Zeb nodded. He wondered what Antonio's eyes looked like in the throes of passion. Did they change color? Did they turn dark and stormy? Would he always want to lose himself in them?

He shook off these thoughts. He wanted Antonio. Badly. The truth was he had no right to claim him. He had no job, no money, no identification. He was a man without a country . . . he couldn't even return to the US with Antonio if it ever came to that.

"You look worried. Are you in terrible pain?" Antonio had stopped eating.

"No. I'm not."

"But how do you feel? Really? You just kicked out the devil. Do you feel lost . . . or found?"

"I feel happy I chose to be here. Antonio . . . I—"

He was interrupted by the arrival of the local doctor who

waved off Antonio's offering of money.

"I heard you were beaten," the doctor said. "The priest says you saved the relic. How can I charge you?" He began to poke and prod. "You have no broken bones, but I see a lot of bruises. No walking for you for a few days. When you do walk, I will bind your feet for extra support."

"You must do this a lot," Antonio said.

"The feet always hurt the pilgrims." The doctor said he would check on Zeb the next day. "Little steps," he said. "Just to the bathroom. Señora Rodriguez will look after you."

He wanted a bath. More than anything he wanted to feel clean. The old lady insisted she would make the water nice. At least that's what he thought she said. When she came back twenty minutes later, she smelled of lemon and oddly, lavender.

Antonio helped him into the bathroom. It swirled with steam and when he looked into the tub and saw the mesh bags of herbs and lemons dangling from the taps, he realized she really had made the water nice.

She left the two men alone when Antonio said he would help him.

"I hope that door has a lock," Zeb said as he began peeling off his clothes. They smelled terrible. Now that he thought of it, he'd been wearing the same things for days.

Antonio was swift to close and lock the door, easing a now naked Zeb into the warm water. Zeb leaned back, enjoying it.

"Relax," Antonio urged, kneeling on the floor beside him. He reached for a washcloth and soap the landlady had left for them. He bathed Zeb with a tenderness that touched him so much he forgot to breathe.

"Why are you crying?" he asked Antonio. It hurt like hell to lift his arm, but he raised it from the tub to touch the other man's face.

"I can't bear to see you in so much pain."

"I've been in worse pain."

"You have?"

Zeb drew Antonio's face to him. "I know I probably taste bad, but I need to kiss you."

Antonio grinned. "You don't. You taste of cake and coffee."

They kissed, Antonio's hand falling on Zeb's now hardening cock.

He leaned back on his haunches, breaking off their mouth to mouth contact. Desire and fear gleamed in his eyes.

"You don't have to—"

"I want to." Antonio's fear slipped away, uncertainty hovering just behind.

Zeb watched the man's face dip down. At first he licked Zeb's cockhead, a huge smile coming to his lips.

"This feels so good," Antonio said, then began moving down. His face hit the water as he sucked on Zeb's cock. Zeb arched his back up to give Antonio better access.

"I'm no good at this," Antonio said, his face looking miserable as he rose from Zeb's cock.

"No good? Do you see how hard I am? Please . . . suck it. It's all I think about. Ever since I caught your dream, I've wanted you. I've wanted to pleasure you."

"If I do something wrong, will you tell me? I don't want to hurt you."

Zeb's heart almost burst with emotion for this man. "You could never hurt me."

"I've never done this before . . . except in my dreams." The smile came back to Antonio's face. Zeb touched it with gentle fingers, his own pleasure rising again after they exchanged hot kisses and Antonio went back to his task.

He sucked and licked. "Open your mouth a little wider so I don't feel your teeth," he instructed in a soft voice.

Antonio nodded. He sucked and slurped with such giddy delight his enthusiasm alone made Zeb come fast.

"A hot bath and a hot mouth do wonders for a man," Zeb said when Antonio worked hard to swallow the explosion of white fire that erupted from Zeb. The orgasm left him feeling better than he had in a long time. He reached for Antonio.

"Get in."

"You came too soon, and I didn't swallow it all."

"It's not a contest, Antonio. You made me feel very good, I promise you."

He dragged the other man over the edge of the bath and into his arms, pain inside them be damned. Water sloshed everywhere, but Zeb didn't mind. They laughed, trying to keep quiet. The landlady walked outside the door.

"I think she suspects something," Zeb whispered as his lips closed around Antonio's cock. It was too hard to suck him in the tub, so he urged the man out of the water. He was so desperate to suck him off he put him on his back on the bathroom floor on top of one of the clean towels their hostess had left for them.

Hovering between Antonio's open legs, he knelt, kissing the man who looked even better naked than fully clothed. As he kissed his way down Antonio's body, he saw the splinters still imbedded in his knees.

"Fuck. That bastard hurt you and I no longer have the power to heal you." he was suddenly desolate. "I have nothing to offer you, no right to you. I have no money, no name . . ."

"Please suck me," Antonio said.

Zeb moved down the man's slim, wet body. He tasted of herbs and soap.

"You tasted so good," Antonio suddenly whispered.

Zeb couldn't respond. His mind was on the huge, hard cock in his hand. "If we do this, it changes everything."

"I no longer wish to be a priest." There was a slight tremor in Antonio's voice, but Zeb knew enough about men to know the poor man was wracked with desire. He began to suck Antonio's cock. It didn't take too long for Antonio to come. He came hard, flooding Zeb's throat. Zeb stayed on him. He wanted the first time Antonio came in another man's mouth and not his own hand to be explosive.

Antonio bucked and moaned, unleashing a small strangled cry. Zeb held on to him, licking up what drops of juice had escaped his greedy mouth and started all over again. He stroked Antonio's rising ass cheeks as he met each sucking and pulling motion from Zeb.

"I want to suck you, too," he murmured.

Zeb lifted his mouth for one tiny moment. "Shhh," he said and went straight back to work. This time, when Antonio came, Zeb swallowed it all.

"Hey, what do you know?" he said, when he released Antonio from his mouth, "it really is like riding a bicycle. It's a long time since I did this, but it's all coming back to me."

"I don't want to hear about the others." The tremulous smile on Antonio's face ripped at Zeb.

"There are no others. Only . . . a lifetime of preparation for you." He covered Antonio's face with kisses.

They set out two days later for the next leg of The Camino to Puente la Reina, Zeb feeling more or less normal. Antonio had bought a few items of clothing for him, toothpaste, and good walking boots. He'd also found him a second-hand backpack at the grocery store that the owner donated when he found out it was for the man who'd saved the relic.

As they studied the walking map, trying to plan their day, a young man came up to them.

"Are you the man who saved the Holy relic?" he asked in broken English.

Zeb felt his cheeks flush. "Um . . . yes, I am."

"They tell me you were assaulted. I am assuming your

pilgrim passport was taken, so we are giving you a new one." He handed it to Zeb who was delighted to receive it. "It's stamped for Obanos and we have alerted the office in Puente la Reina to expect you."

"That's so nice," Zeb said. "Thank you."

The man handed him a small wad of bills. "People have been concerned about you. Señora Rodriguez told us you were getting better each day and that you planned to leave today. People donated to you."

Zeb was stunned at the kindness of strangers. "It is I who should be donating to you. I know most of the pilgrim offices are staffed with volunteers."

"No, no," the man said, backing away. "It is my pleasure." He gave Zeb a brilliant smile and ran back to his office.

"We need to get you a wallet," Antonio said.

Zeb couldn't believe he had money and a pilgrim passport. He smiled at Antonio. "I will treasure these things. And yes, we should buy a wallet."

He longed to kiss Antonio. For the past couple of days they had done nothing but eat good food, kiss for hours and suck each other's cocks. They couldn't keep their hands off one another.

They set off for the road to Puente la Reina, just a mile away and beyond that, the next stage of Estella, which was another eleven miles farther. They had no time constraints and neither man was certain how Zeb would fare. From Puente, the road was mostly uphill, so they planned to take their time.

"My biggest concern is finding some place private to show you how much I want you," Zeb said as they passed fields of corn and wheat. Zeb was using Antonio's walking poles and his feet felt good.

He and Mrs. Rodriguez had spent an hour taking the splinters out of Antonio's knees and shins. They'd had a hard time explaining them to her. Zeb felt so protective of the man, but he'd checked his lover's legs that morning and they were healing just fine. Both men wanted to be together. They wanted to walk and think. Both had questions about their futures.

They arrived in Puenta la Reina, had their pilgrim passports stamped and kept moving.

"Are you sure?" Antonio asked him. He had the anxious look on his face again.

"I am very sure. I'm thinking wherever we stay tonight, let's not go to an *albergue*. I want a nice big, double bed in a room that locks so I can hold you all night."

Antonio grinned at me. "And fuck me, I hope."

Zeb laughed. "If you insist."

They walked, at peace with one another, stopping to rest whenever they felt like it, but it was the least interesting portion of The Camino, just as the guidebooks said it was. They stopped in two small towns for coffees and sandwiches. When they reached Estella late in the afternoon, the town, low in a valley, was surprisingly hot and humid. There were no hotels or rooms catering to pilgrims, but there was a very clean *albergue*. The town itself had been created as a gift to pilgrims in the year 1090 by the King Sancho Ramirez.

"He didn't have a romantic heart," Zeb said, as they took in the two narrow beds in the hostel dormitory they shared with six others.

"Why do you say that?" Antonio asked, peeling off his boots.

"He should have put in a nice big hotel with double beds."

Antonio laughed. "I love you, Zeb."

Zeb looked at him. Antonio's face went bright red. "I mean—"

"I love you, too," Zeb said. He caught the smile of one of the other men in the room. "I have to kiss him."

The other man shrugged.

Zeb kissed his lover. Waiting was totally exquisite torture.

CHAPTER FIVE

They set off early the next morning, Antonio feeling beyond excited. "This hostel serves breakfast!" he told Zeb, who seemed much better today. "None of the others serve breakfast."

Zeb grinned. "I think it's only coffee and bread, my love."

"Yes, but I'm so hungry. We fell asleep last night. Think we'll find a hotel tonight?"

Zeb laughed. "We'd better. I do love how you and I think on parallel lines." They swapped a kiss full of malicious intent and headed into the communal dining room. Antonio noticed Zeb slipping a few euros into a tin cup on the counter. He liked that Zeb was generous.

They helped themselves to coffee, thick chunks of warm bread and blackberry jam.

"Can't we stay?" Zeb moaned as he bit into a second chunk. "I like it here."

"Me, too." Antonio looked over the guidebook. "We have to stop at the magical wine fountain."

Zeb grinned. "There's a magical wine fountain?"

"Absolutely. Instead of water, it pours wine. A gift for us pilgrims."

"We'd better be careful. I'll really not be responsible for my actions if I drink wine."

Antonio laughed. They picked up their gear, thanked the staff and walked toward the town of Los Arcos. Plenty of travelers were already there. Though the legend was fanciful, the reality was that the 'fountain' had been built into the outside walls of the winery, Bodegas Irache. The wine was a gift for the pilgrims.

And boy, it was delicious. They took turns drinking out of paper cups provided. They filled two up when the staff appeared with new cups. They thanked them and kept walking, sipping as they progressed toward their next stop. They passed a small town that intrigued them but by now they were hungry, and they hurried to Villamayor de Montjardin where they ate hearty lunches of sandwiches and slices of cream cake. They bought bottled water after being told that the next nine miles had no other food and that the roadside water fountains were not very good and possibly polluted.

As they walked, the day darkened.

"We may not make it to Los Arcos tonight and there's only an *albergue* there. It's not supposed to be a good one," Zeb said. "They say it's very noisy and I am so disappointed they have no magical wine."

Antonio laughed. He loved Zeb's sense of humor and he didn't care where they slept. "If we find some place nice, with a bit of shelter, I'd be happy with that. I want to be in your arms tonight."

Zeb stopped walking. He threw down his walking poles and took hold of Antonio, kissing him deeply.

"Then that's what we'll do," he said.

They walked past some beautiful stretches of road, then nondescript, wide open spaces. It was a strange day, the sky overcast, and yet, Antonio had never been happier.

"You're not like most humans," Zeb said. "I haven't seen you touch your cellphone once. I've seen some of the guys in cafes freak out. There was also that woman who screamed because she missed out on an eBay auction."

Antonio grinned. "Yeah, that was funny." He shrugged. "There's nobody I want to speak to, except you."

Zeb kissed him harder. "Come on," he said. He bent down,

picked up his walking poles and took Antonio by the hand. They veered off the trail to another jagged walking pathway that seemed to take them up a hill.

"You can manage this?" Antonio asked.

"Yes, I can manage. I have to manage. I have to be in good shape to keep up with you."

Antonio laughed as Zeb pushed him against the trunk of a huge olive tree. They began to kiss, slowly sinking to the ground. Zeb opened his backpack, extracting the big fluffy sweater he'd been given by one of the guys at the *albergue* in Estella since the guy said he'd brought too much stuff with him. It fit right under Antonio's ass. He was astonished at his lover's urgency and at the feelings of arousal that swept through him as drops of rain began to fall.

"God is angry that I am about to fuck his favorite priest," Zeb said, moving up to kiss him.

"No. God's crying with happiness."

Both men laughed. Antonio was relieved when Zeb removed his walking boots, tugged down his jeans and underpants and began licking and sucking his cock and balls. He loved it when Zeb sucked his ass. He'd had no idea how magical it was when that happened. Better than magical wine.

Zeb sucked and licked and rose up to kiss him, before standing and removing his own clothes and boots.

"Hurry," Antonio whimpered. "I need you." He was so afraid of somebody coming before he could get Zeb's cock inside him.

Zeb made a low, growling sound and dropped back down, naked, his cock jutting out as he took Antonio's ass in his hands. He licked and sucked him slowly. "I wish I had lubrication," he said.

"We're pilgrims. Men in ancient times didn't use lubrication," Antonio said. "Lubrication is for lazy people. I want to feel you working your way into me."

"I don't want to hurt you."

Antonio smiled. "Just fuck me."

He almost changed his mind a couple of times, the pain was so great. Each time it got bad, just with his lover's cock head poking inside him, Zeb withdrew and licked him some more. He took his time and when he finally got a little more of his cock inside, Antonio felt the pain shoot from white fire to red to green. An explosion of fire and steam fused in his brain. He couldn't speak or think as Zeb moved in and out of him. The sensation of agony, coupled with a fierce and instant wave of intense pleasure, took him over.

When Zeb muttered in his ear that he loved him, Antonio wanted to respond. He felt his lover's balls slapping against his ass and passion replaced all pain. His legs opened up and Antonio came with a wild cry, the rain pouring down on them.

Zeb's cock pulsed inside him, shocking Antonio. He had no idea it would feel like this, that he would feel every thrust and tremble so deep in his belly. His mouth hung open as he felt a second surge of pleasure, only this was a shared wave. He was experiencing Zeb's release and his arms tightened around the man above him.

"I love you," he shouted. "I love you, Zeb!"

If God hadn't meant for men to fuck each other, for Antonio to love Zeb and to feel his lover's orgasm within him, he didn't think he would have let all this happen.

The rain lessened but fell consistently. Neither man cared. Zeb stayed inside Antonio until he fell out, his cock soft.

Zeb wrapped himself around Antonio, stroking the rain from his face.

It felt humbling and somehow Holy, to make love to Antonio. To be privileged to be his man. Zeb had only ever loved one other person so much. She was gone from him and it made him sad. He was happy, but sorrowful. He knew he wanted to be with Antonio, no matter what the future held.

The rain stopped, they sat under the tree, half-naked, Antonio in his arms. They dozed on and off. Zeb wasn't surprised when night fell, and Antonio asked him under cover of darkness about his deal with the devil.

"Why did you make your pact with him?" Antonio asked. "I won't judge. I simply want to understand."

Zeb tightened his arms around Antonio. "The devil gave me a choice. My mother was sick. She had a bad heart. She was in the hospital. She kept dying. The doctors didn't know how to save her. She would come back, then die again . . . it was awful. The devil didn't want my father, in spite of the fact my father became a very wealthy man from the healings I did."

"That's terrible." Antonio sat up. "Did you make money?"

"I was my father's prisoner. It was a different world then. I was kept hidden from the world. I—"

Antonio was incredulous. "He gave you a choice and you chose to let your mother live?"

Zeb nodded, his eyes seeking out Antonio's in the darkness.

"Did she know you were being mistreated?"

"No, she'd been sick for a long time. I never wanted to bother her. I wanted her to walk again, but the devil drove a hard bargain."

"And he tortured you and punished you . . . then banished you to the wilderness."

"Yeah."

"Where did you have sex?"

Zeb hesitated. "It's the one thing you get to enjoy in hell. Sex. That's why some people choose it."

Antonio shook his head. "I don't want to know."

Zeb grinned. "I didn't love them. I just had sex."

"You're an angel, that's what you are," Antonio said. "You're an angel."

"No. Raphael's an angel. I'm . . . I'm human."

"How long ago did this happen?"

Zeb shrugged, grateful when Antonio nestled himself in his arms again. "About a hundred years. Hope you don't mind our age difference."

Antonio laughed. "You're pretty hot for an old guy."

Zeb loved Antonio's laughter. It was the sweetest sound. The two men talked until the sun rose. They would keep walking. They would finish The Camino. They wanted to be together. No matter what.

Chapter Six

In the days that followed, they walked from town to town. They talked about everything. All the fears they had seemed so insignificant. If they couldn't return to the US immediately, they'd stay in Spain for a while. They finished The Camino going back to Pamplona.

Being the biggest place, they figured they might be lucky enough to find work. Zeb had run out of money, but Antonio still had his savings. In their hearts, they wanted to be together and figured the future would take care of itself. Zeb wanted to teach history since he felt he had a good grasp of that. It seemed like a fantasy to him, the idea of going back to school to receive a formal education.

Antonio wanted to teach music. He loved music. He loved noise.

Back in Pamplona, they checked into a beautiful little hotel. They finally got their double bed. After an intense night of lovemaking, they awoke to music outside in the square.

Zeb gazed out of their picturesque balcony windows. "A bunch of pilgrims are playing their guitars. Let's go down there."

"Okay," Antonio agreed.

Zeb sloped off to the bathroom. Soon, Antonio heard him turning on the taps for a shower. He decided to let his man enjoy his shower in peace. It had been a while since he had checked in with the outside world, his old reality, and he needed to contact the Monsignor and his parents. He'd been charging his cellphone all night. He plucked it from the wall.

He fiddled with it, checking for messages when it rang. It surprised him. He hadn't heard the phone ringing for so long. He'd been in a different and much more beautiful world.

"Mom," he said, actually pleased to hear from her. She babbled about how she'd almost called Interpol when they couldn't find him.

"Where are you? What's going on?"

"I'm in Pamplona. Oh, Mom . . . I'm not going back to the seminary."

"Oh, thank God! Wait. Is that the right thing to say?"

He laughed. Zeb came out of the shower, a towel wrapped around his waist. He looked so gorgeous Antonio wanted him on the spot. He grabbed the towel, dragging it from his lover's hips. Zeb's cock boinged appreciatively. Antonio captured it for a moment with his greedy lips.

"Yes, Mom. It's the right thing to say." Zeb grabbed his cock, rubbing it against Antonio's laughing face. "Mom, I met somebody."

"Somebody?" She sounded so excited.

"Somebody I love." He looked up at Zeb. Their eyes locked. "A lot."

Zeb knelt beside him, covering his face with kisses.

"I love you. I love you," Zeb kept saying.

"Oh, it's a man. I knew it. Antonio . . . is that why you went to the seminary? You thought I'd hate you being gay?"

Antonio drew a breath. "I . . . I suppose I did. I don't know. I—"

He could hear her talking in the background to his father. "We want to see you. We want to meet him. What's his name?"

"Zebediah. And he's the most handsome man in the world."

She laughed. "Of course he is. When are you coming home?"

"He has a little passport problem."

"We'll come to you. We've missed the Running of the Bulls, but the August music festival is coming up."

Antonio grinned, thinking of the music outside. "I think it's already started."

"I'm going online now to make our reservations. Keep your cellphone on." She paused. "What kind of passport problems?"

"He doesn't have one . . . it kind of got lost."

"We'll figure it out. Kiss him for me, okay?" She ended the call.

Zeb's gaze seared into his. He got between Antonio's naked thighs, his lips touching Antonio's cock.

"You heard what your mother said. She wants you to kiss me."

Antonio laughed. He kissed him. "She's coming here."

"Yes, I heard."

Antonio grimaced. "She likes to take photos."

Zeb began to kiss his way down Antonio's body. "I don't mind that."

"She likes to do things as a family."

"Sounds good to me." He kept kissing, arriving at Antonio's rigid cock. He pushed him back on the bed, his mouth engulfing Antonio in one swoop.

"She likes game night and show tunes."

Zeb's mouth stopped moving. He came off Antonio's cock for a moment.

"Show tunes?"

Antonio gazed miserably down at the man now encircling his head and shaft with his insistent tongue.

"Yes. Her favorite show is *The Fantasticks*."

Zeb grinned, swallowing Antonio's cock again. He sucked with just the right amount of pressure, coming off again. "We need to download the album on iTunes. I need to learn all the lyrics." He gave Antonio a wicked grin. "I want her to love me."

He began to suck again, his fingers moving to Antonio's ass. He came off Antonio again to lift his legs. The sweetest sound in all the world was Zeb sucking his balls and oh, mercy, his cock and ass. Antonio gave himself up to the sensations of pleasure. It was better than any dream.

When Zeb lifted his face and moved up to the bed between Antonio's open thighs, Antonio couldn't speak. He had no idea if it would always be this way, this mute need, this desire for immediate release with this man. He saw the same thing in Zeb's eyes. His lover entered him quick and hard. The small moment of pain was swamped by sheer and utter bliss. They kissed each other, their mouths attacking as they came together. It was over too soon. It always was. They showered and dressed and got ready to go hunt down some breakfast. Zeb reached for his hand and kissed it. It was hard not being able to touch each other in public, but they could always come back for a siesta. Now they were in no hurry to plot their next step of the journey, they walked as close together as possible.

Antonio's cellphone rang. It was his mother. "We're coming tomorrow," she said. "And don't worry, we'll help you with Zeb's passport situation." She blew kisses in his ear.

Zeb. His mother was already calling him Zeb. She gave him the flight details and he jotted them down.

"I can't believe you thought I'd be upset that you're gay," she chided. "I was a model. *All* my best friends are gay, darling."

He laughed, then noticed the man from the pilgrim office from his stay at the very beginning of The Camino. The man came running out to him with the brown leather wallet he'd found on the ground and turned in to him.

"Señor!" the man called out, but it wasn't to Antonio he was speaking, but Zeb. "Señor, your wallet!" He handed it to

Zeb who took it, looking stunned.

"Mine?" he asked, but the man was gone. Inside was a passport. An American passport. The name inside it read *Zebediah Raphael Theodore Hope*. Both men were overcome with emotion. The photo looked just like Zeb and there was a passport stamp issued at Pamplona for that day.

"What is it?" His mother asked. He had forgotten she was on the other end of the phone.

"The pilgrim office just found his passport," Antonio said, looking up at the sky and mouthing *Thank You*.

"God works in mysterious ways," she said.

Yes, He did. He watched the gentle way Zeb tucked his pilgrim passport into the wallet, carefully putting the whole thing in his back pocket.

Zeb looked at him as he ended the call. "Mind if we skip breakfast, babe? I feel the need to celebrate with you. In private."

Antonio didn't mind. At all. They turned and retraced their steps, fingers linking. Antonio didn't care who saw them holding hands. He'd found his way. Like so many countless pilgrims before him, The Camino had helped him find his path. At last.

ABOUT THE AUTHOR

A.J. Llewellyn is the author of over one hundred published gay erotic romance novels. He lives in California, but dreams of living in Hawaii. Frequent trips to all the islands, bags of Kona coffee in his fridge and a healthy collection of Hawaiian records keep this writer refuelled. A.J. loves male/male erotica, has a passion for all animals (especially the dog, the cat and the turtle). A.J. believes that love is a song best sung out loud.

You can contact him via email at aj@ajllewellyn.com

www.ingramcontent.com/pod-product-compliance
Lightning Source LLC
Chambersburg PA
CBHW070535130626
46555CB00003B/1433